THE CASE OF THE PURLOINED PAINTING

The Case of the Purloined Painting

Carl Brookins

North Star Press of St. Cloud, Inc.
St. Cloud, Minnesota

Copyright © 2013 Carl Brookins

ISBN 978-0-87839-708-2

All rights reserved.

First Edition: September 2013

This is a work of fiction. Names, characters, places, and incidents are the products of the author's imagination or are used fictitiously. Any resmeblance to actual events or persons, living or dead, is entirly coincidental.

Published in the United States of America

Published by
North Star Press of St. Cloud, Inc.
P.O. Box 451
St. Cloud, Minnesota 56302

www.northstarpress.com   North Star Press - Facebook   North Star Press - Twitter

Dedication

This story is dedicated to my wife, Jean, my traveling companions, Kent and Ellen, my editor, Mary, and my new friends at North Star Press. They, with patience and good humor, helped me make this story better. Further, I want to recognize the hundreds of women and men around the world who are still working to find and restore the art and other treasures stolen during the war in Europe.

Chapter 1

Three men, all heavily bundled against the cold wind and snow that blew down the river and swirled across the stones stood pressing the railing, rigid and stiff, shielding their faces from the biting air. Close together. But not quite huddled. Anger and tension radiated from their positions. Staring each other in the face. Two of them, side by side against the third, the shortest one. "You have it. You must have it on your person. Give it to me now." A harsh demanding voice quickly lost in the growling wind.

The tallest man, lean, his face partially covered by the wide floppy brim of an old-fashioned fedora pulled well down on his forehead against the elements, spoke with a guttural accent. His tone was sharp, low, as if he was afraid of being overheard, even in the midst of the snowstorm on a lonely bridge. He raised a hand to hold the brim of his hat. His companion, several inches shorter, a bulky dark mass, shifted slowly shuffling through the thickening carpet of snow until he was just off the shoulder and to one side of the third, the one they had confronted. A heavier blast of snow swirled down the sidewalk.

The response from the shortest, wiry appearing even in winter wraps, the man who'd been stopped, was hard, belligerent, but oddly hesitant. "Where's what? Who are you? What do you want of me? I don't know you, any of you. Just leave me alone. Did you call? Are you the ones?" His accent became more pronounced as his agitation grew. He leaned forward and shifted his shoulders as if about to take a step. The tall man seemed to brace for an impact.

"Dummkopf! Just give us the ledger und we leave you be."

The confronted man shifted then, tried to step back, away from the two who had blocked him. The third man, the bulky silent one, shifted forward, chest out to prevent separation. He trapped the short man against the stone railing, pressing closer. "Get away from me!" The stocky man began to twist. His cloth cap flew off, lost in the wind and the snow. "I don't know what you think I have, whatever it is you want! I haven't got it." His words were ripped away and flung into the void by the biting wind.

The silent one bent slightly, grabbed the stocky man and as they struggled, pinned his arms. The tall man ripped at the other's coat, throwing it open to the wind. He pawed at the short man's breast. At his pockets. A raised elbow sent a dark stocking cap off into the storm. Gloved hands ripped at the short man, then he abruptly recoiled with a jerk. Suddenly in a moment both frozen in time and exploding with movement, partly obscured by a snow squall, the short man rose up, first on tiptoe, his coat flapping in the wind, the noise lost in the tumult. He tried to fend off the hands grasping his arms, his waist, urging him off the pavement. He leaned, back arched over the concrete parapet, and flailed off into the void. He made no cry as he disappeared in the darkness. The tall man and the other paused for a second, peering over the railing. Then they turned almost as one and, hunched over against the gale, trudged off the bridge back the way they had come. And disappeared. Another snow squall dimmed the glow of the city and muffled their going. Snow swirled into their footprints, obliterating all evidence of their passing.

After several frozen moments, a pale slender figure, almost invisible in a long white hooded coat with a big fur border and a skirt that reached the snowy street, rose from a crouch across the bridge on the opposite sidewalk and shuffled over the slick snow-swirled roadway. The figure paused, then bent to the place where the open stone railing met the pavement. A well-gloved hand reached out and brushed snow from a small pale object in a drift of snow where it lay against the base of the railing. The slender figure, bent low against the storm, plucked up the object and shuffled off along the curved stone bridge toward the dark eastern side of the river, soon lost in the building storm. In minutes, thick snow covered the area and nothing visible remained of the brief drama.

Chapter 2

"Your name is?"

"Is this necessary?"

"Yes, it is. I need some minimum information. You should understand that anything you tell me is confidential, right? Including my files." I peered expressionless at the guy sitting on the other side of my desk. Late winter afternoon gloom penetrated the two windows of my office, building muted shadows in the corners.

"That's bullshit and you know it," he muttered.

"All right. Give me a phony name. It doesn't matter and I don't care."

"Robert Gehrz."

"Okay, Mr. Gehrz." I printed it on my pad. Robert Gehrz. He didn't spell it for me. "What brings you to my office this cold February day?"

He looked down at me for a moment, thin lips working. He didn't want to be here. He appeared like a lot of my upscale, well-dressed, clients. He looked like he should be striding confidently through the skyways, enjoying a warm, controlled environment, hiring some guy in a truck to move the snow out of his ritzy long driveway so his big Caddy or Lincoln or BMW could get to the street. Or sitting comfortably in his expensive smoking jacket by a nice fireplace fire with a long illegal Cuban cigar in his fingers and a snifter of good golden brandy nearby.

I hadn't bothered to turn on the office lights when this suit showed up. He didn't seem to mind. He was out of his environment and the dim winter afternoon appeared to satisfy him. I pegged the guy as a corporate type or maybe an attorney, a product of good breeding, expensive education. Successful. He radiated money and confidence. A level of power and authority. Yes, definitely a corporate type, in spite of the brief descent into gutter language. He looked well-barbered. His fingers were long, tapered. I had the impression of a well manicured hand. His fingers went with his height. I judged him to stand well over six feet. That put him about a foot taller than me.

I reached out slowly, switched on my small desk lamp. It put a bright pool of light on the polished surface of my desk. The effect was to darken the far corners of the office still more. The silent, dusty, corners. It was a scene from a B movie. I should have been wearing a dark gray fedora.

A sigh, then he leaned forward. Pinned me with his remember-you-are-working-for-me look.

His slender fingers flickered in the lamp light when he gestured. His voice was well-modulated. He spoke in complete unaccented sentences. His language, however, was a little abnormal. My synapses raced about, cataloguing, evaluating. Not a positive statement, could be, not will be. Not am. Difficulty, not danger, not even serious trouble.

I figured he meant whatever this was, his reason for being in my office that afternoon, it was only somewhat illegal. Or maybe, in his mind, just exceedingly private. If word got out it would cost the guy some bread. Some cash. Maybe some image. But it wasn't a career-breaker. Probably.

I raised one eyebrow at him, a move I've practiced. It seems to send a message that we're connecting, that I understand. I wiggled the eyebrow. The right one.

He nodded. Stared at my eyes. I stared back. He nodded again. Then he talked some more.

"Here's the thing. I have a certain . . . reputation . . . to maintain. If this . . . situation . . . becomes public, it can be costly."

"All right."

"I'm in a kind of sensitive situation right now. So I want discretion on your part. If this leaks out I could be in difficulty. Absolute. I realize that can make it harder. Your job." He waved one hand, fingers flashing in and out of the tiny pool of light. Definitely a B movie.

"All right. We understand each other." I leaned forward. Assertive, interested.

"I've been seeing this girl . . . this woman."

"And you're married."

"No, I am not. Please don't jump to any conclusions."

"Sorry." I wasn't, really. Jumping, that is.

"We had a . . . a date, last week. And she missed it. She didn't show up."

"Did you call her?" Master of the obvious, that's me.

"Yes, after a few days. But she's never there to pick up."

"How do you know? Maybe she's avoiding you."

He shook his head. One brief movement. He seemed to know that wasn't the case. "Did you go to her place?" A quick nod.

"What's your arrangement with her? You leave a message and she calls later?"

"Yes, that's it. Only she has stopped calling back. I rarely go to her apartment."

"How long ago was this?"

He was silent for a moment. Either assessing the question or trying to remember an earlier lie.

"A week ago," he said finally. "No, it must have been two weeks ago."

"So you've had no contact of any kind with this . . . woman. For around two whole weeks. Is that right?" I paused deliberately but he gave me nothing. "For how long? Give me a date. The date of your rendezvous. The date of your original date."

"I'll have to look it up." He didn't make a move toward a pocket calendar he might have been carrying. His type almost always carried a pocket calendar.

My instincts said not to mention the police. "You waited a long time to come," I said. Through all this, since he walked in and sat down about half an hour earlier, I had kept my voice carefully calm and neutral. Low key. My movements were slow and supremely non-aggressive. I try to do that with any new non-threatening contact. I'm one calm, cool dude, you see. A small PI with a large reputation. Sean NMI Sean, at your service. Tracer of lost persons, collector of evidence of malfeasance, revealer of fraudsters and thieves. Like that.

Another sigh, then he seemed to come to a decision. His decision was to move forward with this situation. That's what he called it. *A situation*.

We continued the conversation as the room grew even gloomier. The days are short in February in the northern climate. Like the month. Not as short as January right after the winter solstice, of course, but February seems to be one of the depressing months.

I learned that my client, Mr. Gehrz, had a highly stressful job in a highly stressful industry. Exactly what, he wasn't prepared to say, but it paid a good salary and benefits. Perks, he called them. He would pay me in cash, he said. I told him that was all right. But I expected a retainer.

"Yes," he said. Then his hand disappeared into an inside pocket. It was a move that had twice resulted in my being shot at when the disappearing hand reappeared holding a pistol. The first time my assailant missed. The second time the jerk winged me.

I didn't miss either time.

So I flinched when Mr. Gehrz reached for his inside pocket. What he brought out was not a pistol but an envelope, a fat tan heavy duty business-size envelope, the kind with the opening at one end. He tapped the envelope twice on the edge of my desk with his long slender well-kept fingers and then he extracted several pieces of paper. I recognized them instantly as Federal Reserve Notes representing the full faith and honor of the United States of America. Each one he laid down on my desk had a picture of Benjamin Franklin on it. He counted them out, one by one. When he got to twenty he stopped. Then he slid the rest of the bills back into the envelope and returned the envelope to his pocket.

I didn't say anything. I considered suggesting that he be careful in my neighborhood, carrying around all that cash. But then I figured he probably knew that already.

He put his finger tips on the little pile of bills at their edge and slid them slowly through the pool of yellow light from the desk lamp until they were right in front of me.

"A down payment. A retainer," he said and sat back.

"Tell me exactly what you want me to do for that," I said.

"I want you to find the woman, figure out what's going on with her, why she has dropped out of my life and whether she wants to resume our relationship. Report the conversation to me verbally. No reports on paper are necessary. Do this all with the utmost discretion."

"I'll need a name and a description, an address and phone perhaps? Anything you can provide will be helpful."

"I have a picture for you. Her name is Tiffany Market. She's tall, about my height, blond, usually, around thirty. She's good looking but not flamboyant. Tiff is not a model or an actress."

His hand did the disappearing act again and he brought out a wallet. From it he fished a small photograph. It was bent at the corners and I suspected he'd had it for a while. It showed an attractive blond woman, average build, standing on an urban street smiling widely at the camera. It was the kind of picture dozens of amateur photographers make of their friends and loved ones. It was unique in its unremarkableness.

"I'd like that back when you are finished," said Mr. Gehrz.

"I'll make a copy," I said.

I turned my back on him and slid the photograph into my copy machine. Noises and lights and I had an exact color copy. I returned the original to him after quickly scanning the blank back of the photo.

"Write down, her name," I said, handing Mr. Gehrz a fresh tablet of lined yellow paper. "Include her name, her address, and the number you call to arrange a date. Include a few public places you've been together, such as restaurants, clubs, events. Also any other aspects of your relationship you'd care to share. The more I have to work with, the faster I'll be able to solve your mystery, Mr. Gehrz. Please don't forget to include your telephone number."

He eyed me with what I took to be a contemplative look then took the pad I offered and spent a few minutes writing down some information as I had asked. There was a pause and my client turned the pad over and laid it face down on my desk. Then he stood up, straightened his long overcoat and gazed down at me. Definitely over six feet. Maybe I should introduce him to Catherine.

"Let me know if you need more money," he said and turned away.

I didn't get up from my desk. Mr. Gehrz walked to my office entrance and quietly left, closing the door behind him. Gently.

I looked at the pile of Benjamins and the upside-down-pad on my desk and decided I wasn't going to be happy with this case. Then I picked up the pad by the edges and laid it on my copy machine. After making a copy of the page, I carefully tore off the sheet my client had written on and slid it into a large glassine envelope on which I noted the date. The envelope went into my lower left-hand desk drawer. I thought about our conversation. Was this Tiffany person a pro? A prostitute? Blond usually. What did that mean? Maybe the woman was married. Is that why Gehrz emphasized discretion? Maybe this woman didn't want to be found. Gehrz's story was not exactly rock solid.

It was a long time before I again talked with Mr. Gehrz.

Chapter 3

"So you didn't see where the two guys went? After they shoved the one guy over the railing? Are you sure they pushed him over the railing? You didn't notice if they had a car at the end of the bridge, for example? You didn't see anything else of relevance? You sure?" I had a lot of questions my guest sitting across from me couldn't, or wouldn't, answer. First the Gehrz client and now this close-mouthed woman, just a few hours later.

"You didn't call the cops either, I guess."

Her dark hair swung back and forth against her ears when she shook her head. I didn't ask why not. None of my business. We'd probably get to that later anyway. I've learned over the years that when a citizen observes a crime and doesn't call the cops, there's usually something in the citizen's background that made said citizen reluctant to get involved. I had other questions I didn't voice right then. After all, being nosy is part of my DNA. Detectives detect by asking questions, lots of them, often impertinent ones. Even in books detectives ask questions. Especially in books. Successful detectives also know when to and when not to ask certain questions.

"It's an interesting story, Anne?" I put a question mark there in my voice because when she came into my office and I asked her name she told me to call her Ann, or Anne. She didn't spell it. The obvious implication being that Ann or Anne might not be her real name.

"It must have been a horrible experience, but I don't know what you want me to do about it. Other than call the cops."

"Here," she said. She had a low throaty voice, probably from smoking, or drinking, or both. Or maybe she was born with it. Or maybe she'd gone to a lot of trouble to cultivate it. Other than her voice, which you could call sexy, I suppose, she was one of the most ordinary looking souls you could ever see. You wouldn't. See her. You'd pass her on the street a dozen times and never remember her. An unremarkable woman of early middle years with nice ankles appropriately dressed for the season. That was it. I knew she had nice ankles because she took her high boots off when she sat down in my visitor's chair. Gave me a flash of smooth calf under her long skirt. Her toenails were painted pale red.

"And you say this incident on the bridge happened three days ago."

She dipped into her unremarkable purse and pulled out a newspaper article torn from a page in our local daily, the *Star Tribune*. It told the story of the discovery of a body in the ice and detritus of the Mississippi River, a few hundred yards down river from the new I-35 freeway bridge. I didn't tell her I'd already read the article.

"This is him," she said. "It's got to be."

I took the article and looked at it. What it reminded me was that the body recently discovered on the ice of the Mississippi River was of an elderly man named Manfred Gottlieb. He'd worked as a back-office supervisor for a medium-sized department store in Minneapolis until his recent retirement. His wife had died years ago and there were apparently no children. Mr. Gottlieb did have a much younger relative who lived in Chicago. It was too soon for an autopsy report in this edition of the paper, and the only remarkable thing so far was the faint series of numbers tattooed on one forearm. Mr. Gottlieb had been in a Nazi concentration camp during World War Two.

I looked up from the article and gave Anne or Ann my best P.I. interrogator stare. Actually, my friend and sometime partner, Catherine Mckerney, says I do the stare quite well. She says it was one of the things that attracted me to her. "A man who can do that look," she told me one time, "has intriguing potential."

I've had lots of practice, having been an active private investigator for a couple of decades. So I gave my visitor my best stare and after a couple of beats said, "After the two men left, you just went on, the opposite way, across the Tenth Avenue Bridge. Yes?"

"Yes," she said. "I kept going the way I had originally been headed."

"You didn't walk across the street and look over the rail down at the river? You didn't look around to see what else there might be to observe?"

"No. As I told you I was afraid the men might come back. I'd be seen. For all I know they had already noticed me or maybe they were following me. Or maybe they decided to come back. I just left. I was nervous. I went off the bridge the other direction and home."

"Do you do that a lot?"

"Do what a lot?"

"Walk around the city at night in a snowstorm."

Her lips slid into a small smile and her eyes lit up. It was transformative. "Yes, sometimes. Often. I like to walk alone at night."

"Did you notice anything odd or unusual on your way home? After the incident on the bridge?"

She gave me a negative shake of her head. She didn't ask me why I even asked the question, either. I wasn't prepared to answer, if she had.

"Describe the two men, if you please." I watched her think about the question.

She shifted in her chair and looked me in the eyes. "They were older, white, I think. It was dark and snowy. One was very tall and even in heavy clothes he seemed gaunt. The other one was shorter and heavier. He walked like he had muscles. He wore a dark knitted cap, like a watch cap. Both men were bundled up against the storm."

I watched her eyes. They didn't shift. I can make notes on a pad without looking. It's something I practiced. So I was pretty sure she was telling me the truth as she knew it. Whether she was telling me everything was a different question.

"Could you hear what they were saying?"

"Only bits and snatches. But it was obvious they were arguing. The tallest man might have had an accent."

Anne or Ann stopped then. I stared at her in silence for a minute.

"Do you have any evidence, even a vague uneasy sense, that somebody is watching you? Maybe only occasionally?"

She shook her head again. "No, why do you ask?"

I lifted one shoulder. A one-shoulder shrug. "Something impelled you to come to me now, a couple of weeks after this incident on the bridge." I left the implication hanging in the sunny silence of the late morning. Silence can be hard to bear and clients often fill it with information of later use to me. Clues, even. This client said nothing. Well, I'd taken on clients who were even less forthcoming so what the heck?

"What exactly is it you would like me to do?"

"I don't want to be connected to this. I want an intermediary. A cut-out isn't that what you call it? That would be you. I want you to take what I know to the police. That poor guy was murdered, but I'm just not willing to get involved. More than this." She stopped then and bit her lip. The lower one.

"There's always a chance those two might come looking for me. What if they remember something? I have money. I can pay you to maybe find them, or help the cops find them so they can be arrested."

She put her hands back into her purse and fished out a business-sized white envelope, the kind with printing on the inside to conceal the contents. When she opened it I could see bills, money, in it. She kept the envelope partly concealed on her lap. Her long slender fingers brought out five one hundred dollar bills. It didn't look like she'd depleted the contents of the envelope much at all. Anne or Ann laid the bills on the edge of my desk in front of her and then with two fingers pushed them across in my direction. Déjà vu.

"Here's a down payment. I'll pay you this much every week until we get to the end or I decide to stop. Agreed?" She looked me in the eyes again. She had a good stare too.

"Do you want an accounting? A bill? A record?"

She shook her head again. I liked the way it set her hair to swinging. "No. You don't have to write it down, but I want you to tell me everything you do each week when we meet."

"How do I get in touch with you if that becomes necessary?"

"I'm sorry, Mr. . . . Sean? There is just no way for you to call me. Anyway, I doubt it will become necessary." She nodded and looked thoughtful. Maybe she was checking off a mental list. "I'll call you." She cocked her head and seemed to be thinking about it. "Yes, I guess I'll check with you occasionally by phone, and to set up our next meeting." She smiled. She had a pleasant smile.

With that, Anne or Ann with the nice ankles and the pretty dark hair and the pleasant smile, replaced her boots on her feet, shrugged back into her nice but ordinary brown winter coat and left my second floor office on Central Avenue in Minneapolis. I heard the elevator and from my window a few minutes later, saw her emerge from the front door of the building. I watched her step into the street between two parked cars and wave one hand, as if signaling for a cab.

It was no cab that slid up and stopped for her in the slushy street. It was a long shiny black limousine. Given the sloppy state of the streets that winter day, the limo had been recently washed, probably only hours earlier. Anne or Ann pulled open the back door of the shiny limo and disappeared. The vehicle slid back into the sparse traffic and went off—I knew not where. The angle was wrong so I had no chance to read the license plate number.

Things were looking up. I had two clients on one day who were paying me in cash that, were I so inclined, might go mostly unreported. Neither appeared to involve physical danger. I couldn't see any reason to get up close and personal with the guys who may have murdered Mr. Gottlieb and locating a woman who didn't want to be found for the elusive Mr. Gehrz was almost always a relatively easy, if sometimes tedious, job.

The one sure way to avoid being found by anybody is to get off the grid. Totally off the grid. Use cash or barter. Sign nothing, make no contracts, do not fly anywhere. Do not go by train, even if you can find an empty box car. Do not drive a vehicle licensed in your name, especially on toll roads. Avoid going out in public. Move to a rural or small town environment and then move again, occasionally. Limit your personal contacts. Be very much alone. Even so, there are people in our prisons who can tell you it's almost impossible to disappear and remain alive for any great length of time. It is possible to disappear by carefully organizing your death so that the body is never discovered.

I figured a little face time with the cops and some information sharing and Mr. Gottlieb's murderers would be apprehended within a reasonable time frame.

I also had no doubt I would find Mr. Gehrz's girlfriend, if that's what she was. It was just a matter of time and not only am I very good at my job, I'm also persistent.

Chapter 4

"How was your day?" Catherine had just been giving me a blow by blow of another day at her massage school. If that sounds a little condescending, I don't mean it like that. I never do. Catherine knows I am 100 per cent in support of her enterprises, but sometimes, murder intrudes over massage.

I was standing at the kitchen counter building us each a drink. It was late and I was still processing Anne or Ann's appearance in my office earlier. Catherine was across the room putting out some cheese and crackers. I detected by her tone of voice I might not have seemed as attentive as usual to her narrative. That's one of the difficulties of being a high-level man of attention. Particularly when it involves personal relationships. If you slip a little, for whatever reason, your friends notice.

"I apologize, my pet. I suspect I have been a bit distracted the past several minutes."

She turned her head and smiled down on me. It felt warm, her smile. Catherine Mckerney has that ability. Her very presence warms me. Hell, when she walks into a room, even if she hasn't been actively looking for me, she warms me. It was a little unnerving at first, when we were just starting out. I'll be frank. I am aware that good looking women are often attracted to short guys like me. Go figure. And Catherine Mckerney is one good-looking doll. Besides that she's taller than the average babe, being a shade over six feet in her bare feet. Add to that her money, yes, she's a well-paid executive massage therapist with her own school and her own income. So you'd think I'd be more careful when she talks to me.

"I'm sorry, doll, I am distracted, disturbed, even. It's this case."

"Maybe it would help if you'd talk about it."

"Hmm, point taken. I haven't talked to you much about this one, have I?"

"No."

"The basic problem is that my client isn't being as forthcoming as he should be."

"Is he hiding bad stuff, you think?"

"That's what I thought at first. But the more I unpeeled his onion, the less substance there seems to be there."

"Wait. You unpeeled his onion?" Catherine grinned. "It sounds dangerous, dirty, even."

I smiled and sipped the single malt I had just poured myself. "Just an expression. You know most cases are a situation around which facts and actions coalesce until you got this ball of knotted twine or layers of an onion. Then somebody gets frustrated and calls for outside help. Me. My job, much of the time, is to cut the knots, or peel away the levels of the onion to get to the core. The answer."

"And now you're getting to the core and it's slip-sliding away, yes?"

"Your perspicacity is breathtaking," I said sliding over to her side of the couch so I could lay a kiss on her cheek. We had adjourned to the living room ready to absorb the evening news from our local television channel.

"My number one client, Mr. Gehrz, is paying me to find this woman, but I keep stumbling over anomalies. Like is she a blond or something else? Maybe a red-head? He alluded to both or either in our one and only interview. Her age seems uncertain in his mind as well. And if that's not enough, there appears to be a third party wandering around the edges of this thing."

"You mean somebody out there on the fringe, but not connecting with you?"

"Something like that. It's sort of an itch that won't be scratched," I said. "Or like this—every so often I look up like there's another person in the room with me."

"You feel you are being watched?"

"Yeah. Sometimes. Other times it's just this vague sense of unease. As if I'm not doing what I should."

"Ohhh. Ghostly apparitions, yet." Catherine smiled.

"I don't believe in ghosts." I heard me say that and then stopped to consider. True on the face of it, but what about intuition? I often did something or followed an unpromising lead because my gut said to. Sometimes it worked out. Often it didn't.

"How do you know this feeling you have is connected to Mr. Gehrz? Could it be the other case? The one about poor Mr. Gottlieb?"

"Well, I suppose. My gut tells me Mr. Gehrz is the source of my current unease." I shrugged. I do that some times. It comes under the same heading as my vaunted eyebrow lifts.

"Gottlieb seems even odder. The cops aren't getting anywhere. Or, at least they aren't saying so if they are, which is odd in itself. The only thing I know right now is that Miss Anne or Ann says some guy was murdered by a push off the Stone Arch Bridge one dark and snowy night a couple of weeks ago now. Her information is confirmed by the discovery of old man Gottlieb's mortal remains some yards downstream a day later.

"She insists she had no other information except there were two guys who did the deed, one of whom sounded like he might have been German. Her words, not mine."

"Do you think she's telling the truth?"

"Yes, I do."

"All of it?"

"No. I think she isn't lying but she's leaving out pieces of the story. If I can figure out what she isn't telling me and why she's avoiding the telling, maybe I can solve the rest of it, whatever it is."

"Well," Catherine said in a perfectly reasonable tone of voice, "why don't you ask her about it. Her story?"

I sipped my very good single malt and nodded. "Ah, now you have reached the nub of my unease. I haven't heard from the lady for two days."

"She is, to use your cop-speak, in the wind?"

"I guess. There was just the one face to face in my office and then the call two days later. She said she'd call and she did that. Gave me addresses, numbers, contacts. Just what you'd expect. That was last week and since then nothing, zip, nada."

"You have tried to locate her, I assume."

"Indeed I have, my pet. This very morning I tried. Called the cell number she gave me. Not in service. No contract with any local phone service. Her address turns out to be a long-vacant lot, excuse the cliché. The one employment reference I weaseled out of her turns out to be wrong. At least, no one at the company would admit ever hearing her name before. Of course, Target Central is a large company and I didn't talk to every soul who works there, only to ones who would have reason to know the answers." Since I have been in the PI business for a good long while, I have developed many and sundry networks and contacts that almost always produced at least small tidbits of useful information. We call 'em clues, in this business. But my client, Miss or Ms. or Mrs. Ann/Anne Somebody-or-other, had left damn few traces on the ground. Well, to be more accurate, whatever traces she was leaving were, so far, indiscernible to myself.

A sudden warm breath wafted over the side of my neck. A soft murmur crawled into my ears and a very sultry voice I instantly recognized began to suggest things, intriguing things, intimate, even erotic, things. There was even an explicit hint of some sort of lubriciousness that carried an intriguing attractiveness.

We decided to go to bed for a while.

Sometime later, the telephone chimed.

Now, it was getting late in the evening and PI lore to the contrary, I was not in the habit of sortie-ing into the dark streets of Gotham at the beck and call of any old one, known or not. That be said, something told me I'd better answer the call. We have two lines in our shared apartment, one being a private line tied to my business. The other was your regular, garden variety land-line. Catherine also had a cell.

Why, you might ask, in this age of cells, blackberries, cages and pads of various configurations, with the ultimate mobility in communication all around, why we didn't both have cell phones. You may well ask. I make no reply.

I rose gracefully from the bed, wrapped a robe around my nakedness and crossed to the phone. Lifting the receiver, I said, "Good evening, Sean Sean, at your beck and call."

The earpiece hummed and I heard breathing. Then an asthmatic voice said, "I need to talk with you, Mr. Sean. My name is Derrol Madison."

I blinked. Derrol Madison! One of the most expensive and well-thought-of attorneys in the state was calling me. Late in the evening.

Chapter 5

It was nearly noon the next day and I was standing in the skyway over Nicollet Mall when the feeling struck me again. Somebody was watching me, observing my actions. Or maybe just paying mild attention. That's always been one of my useful attributes, an occasional hypersensitivity to being the target of interest. It's saved my life on a couple of occasions. It's nothing paranormal or woo woo, no hairs rising on the back of the neck, it's just a feeling I get once in a while. Whenever it happens, it's usually because I don't seem to be making much progress on whatever it is that's occupying my attention at the time. Occasionally it helps focus my thought process.

Without appearing obvious about it, I hitched myself around so I could look the other way, back toward Macy's department store from whence I'd come. I slid the picture of the woman Mr. Gehrz had given me back into my breast pocket. I'd tried to reach out to Mr. Gehrz because I had more questions. Mr. Gehrz had not responded, a circumstance that was getting on my nerves, just a little. I maneuvered my crutch so I could sag back against the glass wall over the suspended walkway. I didn't need the crutch. It was a prop designed to elicit a little sympathy. It made my frequent stops and slow progress through the skyway more plausible. I didn't appear to be loitering. Loitering was frowned upon, although there was a good deal of it in the Crystal Court of the IDS building. So here I was, watching Catherine, trying to identify who might be watching her. I had, in fact, spent several hours over a few days running surveillances on Catherine's daily comings and goings.

I was probably overreacting. Both Catherine and I had been feeling that way off and on for several days. Observed. Of course she's a spectacular looking woman. I was trying to determine the source of her unease. I was not successful.

It seemed to me the logical conclusion was that somebody I was so far unsuccessful at detecting had been tailing Catherine at the same time I was being watched. A very odd circumstance. Coincidence? Not likely. Since there was absolutely nothing in Catherine's life that would merit such attention, whoever was watching her, it had to be because of our association. Association, such a neutral word to describe our relationship. We'd been a couple now for almost four years. We met first when I did security for an upscale charity thing in Minneapolis. Catherine was a guest. I noticed her because she was tall, the tallest woman in the crowd of five or six hundred. Not only was she tall, she was wearing five-inch heels and an amused expression most of the evening. Elegant. Refined. Attractive.

I learned she owned a successful massage and therapy school in Minneapolis. The following week I made a reservation for a massage. I'm a devotee. When she saw me in the lobby and recognized me, she took the appointment for herself. We hit it off and things have progressed.

I made it a habit to avoid entangling Catherine in my cases. Once in a great while she entangles me in her business life. Our emotional lives are most definitely entangled.

I didn't want her soiled by some of the low-lifes I occasionally dealt with. There wasn't much of that but I also didn't want the occasional psychopath I encounter to endanger her. Most people knew I had a companion, but not who it was or where we hung out.

"Hey, tiger, I almost didn't recognize you. What's with the crutch? Oh." Catherine grinned down at me. Sometimes she found my little subterfuges amusing. Sometimes she helped me with computer searches and was a wonderful sounding board when I needed to talk about my life.

"I came down town to maybe take you to lunch," I said.

She pouted prettily. "Wish I could accept. It seems I have to meet with some lawyer. We're working on a contract for that new accounting operation and they seem not to like something about my standard contract." She put her hand on my shoulder and we moved to one side to avoid the growing crowd passing from the Crystal Court over the busy street below.

"Has your feeling gone away?"

"The one about being observed?"

"That's the one. Right now I'm getting some vibes."

Catherine smiled and scanned the crowd surging around us. It was mostly made up of men in dark suits and women in smart-looking but brighter business wear. "Not me. Your shields must be deflecting the rays. I better get along to my meeting."

A wheelchair broke through the crowd. It was pushed by a dark-complexioned woman in a red blouse with long sleeves. Her skirt was dark blue and long, brushing her ankles. Her hair was done up in a long dark braid that swung back and forth over the head of the man in the chair whenever she leaned forward. The man I recognized.

He was large, somberly dressed as usual in an expensive dark suit and white shirt. He had a dark blue robe across his lap to conceal the fact that his legs were missing below the knees.

I knew attorney Derrol Madison had been injured in a car accident many years ago. It was unusual to encounter him out in crowds of people during the day. Intensely private, he spent most of his time in his office suite in the IDS Tower or his home in an upscale western suburb of Minneapolis.

I was not surprised when he reached over and extended one hand to me. Madison's call the night before was the real reason I was in the skyway. We shook. "Sean," he said with no hesitation and no smile. "We must have a drink some time. I think I'm going to require your services."

His grip was strong and sure. Legless he might be, but he didn't seem to be losing any upper body strength and he appeared healthy. I knew the investigation service he normally used. They were a multi-person office. He and I had occasionally been on opposite sides, but I'd never worked for him.

"You must have my office number," I said. Catherine touched my arm in goodbye and went off on the skyway.

"I'd rather not be on your recorder with this," he muttered and wheeled on by. "Or in either of our appointment books." I glanced up to see Catherine lift one hand, catch my eye and disappear off into the building corridor.

"Here, hang on," I said. I fished out a business card and scribbled a location. "Three today suit you?" He took the card from my fingers and wheeled away with his ever present attendant. Either he'd be there or he wouldn't. It mattered little to me—the bar I'd suggested was on my way home.

Which is all about why I was walking through late afternoon sun on that crisp February afternoon into the Marriott Fairfield Hotel lounge on I-35W just north of the Twin Cities.

The lowering sun was noticeably warmer in color than it had been earlier in the day. Madison was ahead of me sitting with his back to the western-facing windows. The blinds were open and the place was bright. Tables had been shoved aside to accommodate Madison's wheelchair.

I ordered a shot of twelve-year-old Macallan from the waitress who couldn't have been even twice the age of the scotch.

"Not exactly off the beaten path," Madison said.

I shrugged. "It's quiet. Almost no one comes in here this time of day and it's outside your usual haunts. What's the big secret?"

"I'm doing a favor for a friend. That's all. He wants some help, the services of an investigator. I said I thought I could find someone acceptable. That was two weeks ago. I made several suggestions. He talked to some of them. Then we began to have inquiries, inquiries that went nowhere. After a while, I went through the lists and discovered somebody or several somebodies had been finding out about my firm. I didn't like it."

I was beginning not to like it either. We speculated for an hour about who and why his firm was being watched. I didn't tell him about my similar unease.

Madison was on his third whiskey sour since I'd arrived. Clearly, the thing had bothered this experienced attorney in a way he hadn't experienced before.

He glanced around at the dozen or so patrons in the big room. There was no one close, and I didn't see anybody I knew, although that was possible, since we were in my neighborhood, something I was pretty sure Derrol Madison didn't know. Most of his contacts with me, few in number, had been in Minneapolis or by phone.

Madison continued to insist that the name of the friend he was fronting for was of no consequence, had no bearing whatsoever on the situation. What he wanted me to do was meet a man from Chicago. Naturally I wanted to know who he wanted me to meet and why. He still demurred.

"Mr. Madison, with all due respect, I'm a little surprised you want me to handle this task."

He stared at me. "Are you refusing?" Trust a lawyer to look for "innerdeeperhiddensecret" meanings.

"No, sir. I'm happy to accommodate you. I have nothing pressing on my plate at the moment," I lied. "I just wonder why you chose to use my services since we've never done business together before."

"That's it precisely." He took a sip of his drink. Actually it was a rather large sip. Something was bugging the man.

"Ah. You've decided you want a distant relationship, not something for a regular contact."

"You are as perceptive as I was informed."

"All right. I accept your commission, but you'll have to give me a name."

"Excellent. I'll send you the particulars, including the name of the man from Chicago you are to meet." Madison finished his drink and set the glass down with a clack that traveled through the quiet room.

"Well." I stretched my arms overhead and dropped a napkin on the floor in the process. The maneuver not only provided some relief from a little stress in my shoulders, but it gave me a brief opportunity to scan the room behind me. It was almost empty, which made it easier for me to notice and wonder about the solo woman sitting at a table on the far side of the room. "Was there anything else?"

"I have to get going," Madison said, glancing at an expensive-looking wristwatch.

"All right. Do you need any help?"

"Just move the table so I can get out, please."

I did and he rolled his chair away from the window. We didn't shake hands. I stood, drink in hand and watched him roll efficiently to the doors to the lobby which opened as if by magic, but I detected the fingers of a hand pulling the door open. I sat down again to finish my drink and after two trips to the glass I glanced around to note that the single woman customer was no longer in her place.

Chapter 6

"Do you know this woman?" I asked. Ricardo Simon, Minneapolis police investigator, leaned back in his chair and swallowed the last spoonful of the French onion soup he'd had for lunch.

"Thanks for lunch, by the way," Ricardo said, looking down at the picture I'd placed in front of him while mopping a bit of soup from his mustache. The mustache was new. His love of French onion soup, especially made at Le Bistro, was not. Le Bistro was only a block from the cop shop in downtown Minneapolis. Made it handy for him, particularly on a cold and brittle winter day like this one. It was cold, temperatures hovering around zero. I hadn't wanted to come downtown. I hadn't wanted to go to my office, but I did both. Persistent to the cause, that's me. As long as I was out, meeting my friend detective Ricardo Simon for lunch, seemed like a good idea.

The pale February sun was too weak to dispose of much of the winter's grimy snow that lay about the curbs in untidy lumps. We needed either a fresh snowfall or, preferably, a bright hot day to bring melt to the streets. Weather reports were not hopeful.

Simon was a friend of several years. We'd first met when he was a patrolman waiting for the results of the sergeant's exam. He passed with a high score and then waited for a vacancy and the promotion. Not long thereafter he moved to the homicide section where he happily chased killers and citizens who fell into bad circumstances or bad company or both. In the past ten years we had done each other the occasional favor, helping to clean up after some nasties.

"Is this a client?"

"Nosir. This is a picture of the woman the client wishes me to find." I related the story Mr. Gehrz had told me.

"So far, I have come up empties. Some of the people I interviewed at Target where she worked recognized her but said she left after several months, maybe a year at most. Her name, I was informed, is Tiffany, Tiffany Market. She has no driver's license, no known local address, no friends or family, at least none I can find in the public records."

Ricardo peered at the picture. "I think this was taken on Nicollet Avenue, probably last summer," I said.

"Very good. You're right. It's obviously summer or late spring and that construction in the background looked pretty much like that in May and June. They finished the building and repaved the street there in late August."

"That sounds about right."

"I checked," I said, "with the street department. They verified my recollection."

"This picture was supplied by your client?"

"Yep. One Mr. Robert Gehrz."

Detective Simon raised his eyebrows.

I nodded. "Passingly creative, I agree."

"Did Mr. Gehrz give you any reason for concern?"

"Not a whit. He told me she hadn't shown up for a planned rendezvous about two weeks before we met. He stated further that in the past she'd always called him if she didn't make their appointment and he was concerned. He gave me the usual information about her and the usual runaround about himself. I'm not allowed to contact him in any way."

"Cash deal?"

"Of course. A couple of other things. Look more closely at the picture of this woman."

He did, leaning over and peering closely for several seconds. Then he looked up at me. "Odd. There is something odd about this. But I don't know what it is, exactly."

"You're right. Catherine noticed it last night when I showed it to her. I think the facial features have been slightly altered. The other thing that's odd is her general similarity to someone else I met recently."

"Photoshopped, possibly?" said Simon.

"Exactly. Not a whole lot, and maybe not by an expert. I think Mr. Gehrz is not all he seems, nor is his quest quite on the up and up. I admit while enjoining me to absolute discretion, his language, when he described the difficulty he would be in if this search became public, was more circumspect than that, even."

"Circumspect?"

"Yeah, he wouldn't be killed or anything if it all came out, only in some difficulty."

"Strange. Do you think there's a connection between this woman and your new client?"

"No. So on to another topic. Can you tell me anything about the investigation into the demise of Mr. Gottlieb?"

"Not much, but why are you interested?"

"Since I first brought up my other client, the woman who paid me to be an intermediary, you remember, Anne or Ann?"

Simon nodded again. "Oh, right. A mysterious woman who may or may not know something about Gottlieb's death."

"There's been a development. Your friend, attorney Derrol Madison, has been in touch. In a very hush-hush sequence. So I must tell you that this is all on the Q.T."

Simon, who is used to our occasionally convoluted dances in the garden of information sharing, just looked at me and waited.

"Mr. Madison called me late one evening this week to request a meeting. We met briefly in sort of a moving encounter in the Macy's skyway. That in itself was odd, since I'm sure you know he rarely goes out in public. Later that day I met him in an out-of-the-way bar. Never mind where. It was of my choosing and I'm sure it doesn't figure into this.

"Anyway, he told me that he was acting for a friend, or maybe the friend of a friend, who wanted a reliable investigator to help an acquaintance, or a client, or a close friend or . . ."

Simon raised one hand. "I get the picture."

"Tomorrow I will meet this man who is coming here from Chicago. We will go to his relative's home for a look-see." I paused for a sip of water.

"And?"

"According to Madison, the man's name is Aaron Gottlieb. He's the great nephew of Manfred Gottlieb, the man of who we just spoke? The man found dead in the ice of the river."

Chapter 7

I met Aaron Gottlieb the next morning at a big old home on the south side of Minneapolis, per our arrangement. It was one of those shabby stucco two-story single family homes built sometime in the early to mid twenties. In the previous century. It was his grand uncle's home when he died. In fact, Aaron Gottlieb informed me, the place had been owned by Gottliebs since it was built. He wasn't sure whether a Gottlieb had actually built it or not.

His grand uncle was the late Manfred Gottlieb. Aaron Gottlieb wanted my help in finding out how his grand uncle had ended up in the river, confirming what attorney Madison had told me.

The cops hadn't told him much, Gottlieb reported. Was this a suicide or was his grand uncle, elderly but in vigorous good health for someone approaching a century of living, a man who had endured most of World War Two in a Nazi concentration or work camp, helped over a parapet or forcibly tossed in the river? According to the cops, which was according to Aaron Gottlieb, there was precious little evidence of anything, one way or another.

I knew that to be true, more certainly than Gottlieb did. I also knew the answer, if my mysterious client Ann or Anne was to be believed about that snowy confrontation on the Stone Arch Bridge. That's the bridge James J. Hill, the local transportation magnate, had constructed so he could run his railroad, the Great Northern, to the west coast.

I chose, for now, not to share those revelations and speculations with this young Mr. Gottlieb, since neither had the cops. But I wondered why the cops had been so reticent. I also wondered what an eighty-plus-year-old guy was doing in a February snowstorm, wandering so far from home.

Manfred Gottlieb's body had contusions, a couple of broken ribs, a cracked hip and other injuries that could have come from falling off a bridge upstream from where his body was recovered. That had been reported from the medical examiner.

Some of those injuries could have been the result of a beating. One scenario suggested Gottlieb was beaten, died and then was tossed into the river. Another scenario, supported by the evidence, suggested he fell off a bridge, having jumped or been pushed. For Aaron, suicide was simply not possible, ergo, he was leading me to this room where we hoped to find . . . something.

Aaron was afraid that if something concrete didn't turn up, the authorities would slide the case into the unsolved or label it death by mischance, and that would be the end of it.

So now I'm standing in this dim attic, circa 1920 something. It's a perfectly good attic, as those things go. No recent leaks, no paneling, bare wood floor and a real staircase, not a pull-down ladder, to get up here.

My host is the man I just met named Aaron Gottlieb, my referral from attorney Derrol Madison. His grand uncle Gottlieb is the man who fell—or was pushed—off a bridge. The Tenth Avenue or maybe the Stone Arch Bridge. The authorities were not certain which bridge. My information, from the mysterious lady named Anne or Ann, was that the unfortunate Gottlieb was chucked off the Stone Arch Bridge. It happened because he refused to give up some piece of property. His grandnephew, increasingly concerned about this property and the lack of progress in figuring out why his relative had died, had invited me to this address to try to detect what, if anything, might have caused Uncle Manny's death. Aaron explained to me that even though the deceased was Aaron's grand- or great-uncle, he, Aaron, always called him "uncle."

I had promptly reported my information from the lissome Ms. Anne or Ann to the local cops because that's not the kind of thing I ever want to keep to myself. The cops have all sorts of resources I don't have and I never thought we were in some sort of competition to clear cases.

Anyway, here we were, having already been through the whole house except for the two rooms used by a long-term renter. I'd get to him later.

"I have to tell you, Mr. Gottlieb—"

"Aaron, please."

"Aaron—that you shouldn't get your hopes up."

"I know, I get that."

"We have so little to go on right now, we could miss something significant without realizing it."

Aaron nodded again. "I don't know what else to do. Manny was the only family I had left. I think or I hope you'll see something, or anyway, get a better picture of Manny."

"What about your own parents?"

"Both deceased. My granddad was in the war, you know. He volunteered early because we had family in Europe." He stopped talking and stared at the angled wall, actually the underside of the roof. "Manny was one. Of course we had no information, no idea what had happened to my great uncle. Or the others. We still don't. Not entirely."

"Where did your grandfather serve?"

"Army. European theater. He was wounded in 1945 and came back to the states then. He never made it to the ancestral home in Poland."

"Did he ever talk about his experiences? Tell you war stories?"

Gottlieb shook his head. He went to a tall dark brown wooden cabinet. The thing looked old. There was a shiny hasp and padlock attached that secured the door to the frame. Aaron flipped the lock with one finger. "Uncle Manny put this lock on after we persuaded him to take in a boarder so there'd be somebody in the home as he got older and needed more help."

I cocked an eyebrow at him. He was fishing for a ring of keys and didn't notice. "How long did he have renters?"

"About five years, I think. Mostly young women who are grad students at the U. They get a nice room, private bath and kitchen privileges. Cheap. In return, they made him dinners or breakfasts, sometimes both, when they were here. We've had meals on wheels for a couple of years and a home health aide once a week. Sometimes, between semesters, when the renters were gone, neighbors helped out."

"Nice to have such services available," I observed, watching him fiddle with the key ring. He finally found a key that fit.

"Yes. I guess I better put that in the past tense. Difficult to remember. It was hard to convince him he needed help of any kind. About the stories. Uncle Manny, granddad's nephew, survived Birkenau. He would never talk about those years. He told us what he found when he went home after the liberation. The house was wrecked and abandoned. People in the neighborhood said an SS officer and his family had been living there for a year or so."

Aaron removed the lock and swung the cabinet door open. I noted the hinges didn't squeak. I also noted that the hasp had been installed so it could easily be removed from the outside with only a small screwdriver. The padlock was no real security.

"Manny said the house was mostly empty of furniture and there was no electricity or water. The authorities didn't want him to stay there. He packed up some stuff he found in a big trunk and somehow had it shipped to America. The family story is it took most of a year or maybe more before it got here. By then the family knew both dad and granddad were alive and on their way to the U.S. Granddad never showed anybody what he'd packed in the trunk."

"So you never saw the contents, ever?" I found that difficult to believe.

"Hard to believe, isn't it? I opened this cabinet for the first time last week after we sat Shiva for Uncle Manny."

He swung the doors wide so I could see the tightly packed shelves. "I guess you didn't show this to the cops, am I right?"

Aaron nodded. "I didn't see the point. But now, with the chance he might have been murdered, you have to see everything."

"The first time you looked in here, did you go through the contents?"

He shook his head. "No. I guess I felt so sad. And there was so much here. Look at it. Who knows what all this is? I just closed and locked it up again."

"All right," I said. "Let me get some pictures." I unlimbered my digital SLR and photographed the shelves. Then we began to carefully unpack shelf after shelf, riffling through the piles of mostly clothing. Men's clothes. Women's. A bundle that might have been children's. As Aaron took out piles from each shelf or cubby, I slid my fingers in the folds just in case there was something alien to find. Nothing. I didn't say so then but it occurred to me some theater company might be the beneficiary of a lot of nineteen-twenties style clothing in the future.

Aaron said, "Look at this." He was holding a long cardboard tube, sealed at each end. "It's heavy."

I handed him my pocket knife and he carefully slit the cap at one end. It crackled and bits of glue and paper flaked off. Because the stuff had been stored in an attic instead of a basement, there was no damage from dampness or mold, but the cap was dry and brittle. He slid a tightly rolled stash of papers into my hands. Working together we carefully fingered through the leaves. It was a collection of illustrations.

Because the paper was so dry, we didn't unroll the sheets all the way. What we found was a whole series of drawings, some in pencil, some pen and ink. They seemed to be a variety of views, and there were portraits, sketches. Were they valuable? We couldn't tell and it would take some careful expertise to unroll and examine them fully. Aaron decided to replace them in the tube and set it aside for later. I concurred.

While he'd been looking at the illustrations, I peered more closely at the cabinet. Each of the doors hung on three concealed hinges. But the hasp and loop had been installed so that the screws on one side were exposed. My examination suggested to me someone had removed the screws and reinstalled the hasp. The screws were not carefully and completely screwed into the wood. I filed that bit of information away for later.

At the bottom was a drawer half the width of the cabinet. I slid it open. It was filled with stuff, knickknacks, odd tools, coins, pins, nails, small paper envelopes, the kind of detritus that you probably have in a kitchen drawer. An old sewing kit. I lifted out the sewing kit to reveal a small thick cardboard sleeve. It was the kind of hard-board box sleeve sometimes used for limited editions of books. This one was about seven inches by five inches. The brown suede leather box was about two inches thick. Embossed on its surface in gold leaf was a single word. *Beschlagnahmen*. The word was Germanic-looking.

"Is this a family name?" I asked. "Do you know what it means?"

Aaron peered over my shoulder at the box. "I don't recognize it. I never studied German and my family didn't use Yiddish much either. What's in the box?"

"Nothing," I said, turning the box over. The empty brown suede offered no additional clues. "Whatever was in here is gone and that's interesting."

"We can take it to a bookstore or to somebody who deals with old books. Maybe the historical society?"

We set the sleeve aside and went on with our search.

Chapter 8

In the rear corner of the attic room where we had started was a neat stack of four cardboard boxes. They belonged, Aaron told me, to the woman who was renting one of the bedrooms. She was the only renter at the time we were there. I glanced over the top row of boxes, just about at chin level. Each was tightly sealed. The boxes were also slightly dusty. When I peered at my feet, I could see that the boxes had recently been disturbed. There was a line in the film of dust on the floor that told me the stack was not in precisely the same place it had been. I decided not to mention it to Aaron. I wasn't sure why.

After spending a little more time pawing through Manfred Gottlieb's cabinet and finding nothing of obvious interest, Aaron and I descended to the first floor where we decided to examine the extensive bookshelves in what had been a formal dining room at some time in the past.

When I relate that we found nothing of interest in the attic, I should perhaps explain I meant nothing of interest that connected directly to his death. I was also debating whether to tell Aaron about my other client, Anne or Ann NLN (means no last name) who may have witnessed the murder of his grand-uncle. By itself that might not be significant but the old guy was dead under suspicious circumstances and there were questions. So, yes, I wanted to look around the rest of the place as long as I was in the house. And no, I wasn't going to mention my suspicions—at first. I figured Aaron had enough on his plate at the moment and I was certain by now from his attitude and things he'd said that he'd had no hand in the crime. It wouldn't help his state of mind to know I believed someone had been in the attic.

Aaron frowned at me when we went into the next room. "Frankly, I don't get it. What are you looking for now, Sean?"

"Same answer I gave you when you asked the first time, I'm afraid. I don't exactly know, but I'm pretty sure I'll recognize it when I see it."

He nodded sagely. Can you do that? How does a sage nod differ from an ordinary nod? "Okay, how do we proceed? Surely you aren't going to shake out every book in here looking for secret messages?"

I grinned. "You've been reading too many spy novels."

"Well, I have read some Enzo McLeod."

I walked to the nearest case and ran my fingers over the backs of the row of books at eye level. "Ah, Peter May," I said over my shoulder. "My friend Catherine is a crime novel buff. She likes his books. She says he gets it right."

The shelf of books under my fingers were all dusted and in good condition. It was an eclectic collection, all hard covers. There were some classics, a leather bound volume of Shakespeare's plays, some histories and three religious texts. A black bound copy of the Koran, the King James Old and New Testaments, and some Hebrew texts I couldn't read, even after I figured out I was looking at them backwards.

"Those are study texts, in both Hebrew and Polish," Aaron said coming up beside me. "Our family lived in a town that was sometimes Polish and other times German. Politics and border treaties, you know."

The books were shelved in some kind of order, I sensed, but it wasn't clear to me what it was. None of the books were obviously placed incorrectly, upside down, or noticeably out of sequence. Or if they were out of place, which I didn't know, what, if anything, was the significance? The alternative was to ascribe something significant to the fact that the several shelves of books appeared to be exactly where they should be. That is, unlike the stuff in the attic, it didn't appear anybody had searched this room.

As we left the quiet house, I asked, "Aaron, do you know when your roomer will be back?"

He frowned in thought. "Oh, right, you wanted to talk to her, didn't you." He shoved his fingers into a breast pocket and pulled out a piece of note paper. "Here. I called her yesterday to let her know what was going on and that we'd be here today. Her name is Ursula Skranslund. She's a grad student in Linguistics at the U. This is her number. She'll be home tonight if you want to call her."

I took the paper and we parted ways. Gottlieb would return to his hotel, check in with the police about release of the body and a funeral home about his grand uncle's cremation, and then his—Aaron's—return to Chicago. He had a regular job and he needed to get back to it.

"You've got all my contact numbers," he said, "and I've got yours. I won't waste your time bugging you with frequent calls, but please let me know how the case goes."

The Case of the Purloined Painting

* * * *

It being February, darkness was already descending a few hours later as I drove the snowy streets back toward the late Manfred Gottlieb's home and my appointment with Ursula Skranslund. She was home, her slightly accented voice had assured me on the telephone, and would be happy to receive me.

There was a small light over the front door and the sidewalks had been shoveled again. There were lights on in the back of the house that cast a dim glow on the smooth white snow cover at the side of the place. A light shown in a second floor room which I assumed was the woman's. She answered the door after my first ring.

Quite tall, large and well-proportioned was Ms. Skranslund. Her handshake was firm and friendly. She had a thick mane of bright blond hair that cascaded down her back over the gray UofM sweatshirt she wore. Her substantial hips were tightly encased in worn blue jeans. She was barefoot. Ursula led me to the kitchen at the back of the house and into a breakfast nook with two cups already on the table. A pot of coffee was brewing on the stove.

"I have some really fine Arabica coffee, Mr. Sean. I hope you'll join me?"

I nodded yes. Her accent, Finnish, she said, was delightful. I considered asking her to read me something. I didn't, that wouldn't be professional. I pulled out my identification.

"I don't want to alarm you unnecessarily," I said, "but it would be safer for you here alone, to ask for ID before you let a stranger into your house." I smiled.

She smiled back. "You are not exactly a stranger." She brought the pot and poured coffee for both of us. The aroma was heavenly. "I called the number you gave me and then I looked you up on the computer. Then I also called and talked to a very nice woman. Your ... um ... friend? She described you, exactly, including the stocking cap you had on."

So, I thought, sipping very tasty coffee. You found me on the Internet, did you? I'd have to do something about that. But not now.

"I guess you know what I'm here about," I said.

Ursula nodded. "Yes. It was so sad. I like Mr. Gottlieb very much. He made me feel like I was his granddaughter, or a favorite niece."

"I understand you are studying linguistics at the U? And working on a graduate degree in Scandinavian languages?"

She nodded in the affirmative. "And how long have you been renting a room here?"

She frowned prettily. "It has been about eighteen months."

"Have you discussed your situation with Aaron Gottlieb?"

"Oh yes, he and I talked. He called me from Chicago. He is happy to have me here as a sort of live-in caretaker at least until the estate is settled or my lease runs out. That would be next year." She poured more coffee for us. "I see to maintenance and keep the walks shoveled, things like that. He said I can really have the run of the house. I expect Mr. Gottlieb will try to sell the house as soon as he can."

"How did you find this place to rent?"

"I had been sharing a house in Southeast. There were four or five of us at various times. But it became too much a party pad." She paused. "Is that right?"

I smiled. "Yes, a party house, and you wanted more quiet to study, I presume."

"Yes. I saw an ad in the American Jewish World. Mr. Gottlieb and I were um, simpatico right away, you understand?"

I nodded.

"He liked me. I could tell and he liked having a pretty young woman around." Ursula stopped then and frowned. "You must understand. We were friends but it was all very straight, very much business." Her eyes teared up. "Sorry. I miss him."

"I understand. Now tell me about the attic."

"I had some boxes from school and some other things I wanted to keep but not use in my room. We arranged to put them in boxes in the attic. I think there are four, yes? I haven't been up there since we put them there last year."

"Do you remember, were they sealed?"

"Yes, Mr. Gottlieb said it would be better to tape them so he got some sealing tape for me."

"Did you and he carry the boxes to the attic?" I was beginning to think this was a blind alley.

"When I first moved in here I was dating a man and he helped me move."

"Did you see the cabinet in that attic room?"

"Oh, yes. It had hinges and a padlock on it. I thought it was crudely done to a very nice cabinet."

Ms. Skranslund gave me the name of the man who helped her move in and I wrote it in my notebook, although I suspected it would mean nothing in the end. But I would check him out anyway.

Ms. Skranslund accompanied me to the door and we said goodbye. I noticed she seemed relieved when we parted, as if she thought she'd passed some kind of test.

Chapter 9

"My liege?"

I did not respond immediately. My mind was elsewhere.

"Hey," Catherine's voice was closer and more insistent. Moving. A moment and her hot breath was warming my cheek. She'd just come in the door of my house in Roseville. During the winter I made it a practice to spend a couple of days every week, not necessarily in sequence, there, to be sure my resident livestock was fed and watered and that the systems continued to work as advertised. I'm referring to heat, water, electricity and like that.

We'd recently acquired a new tenant, a young chocolate point Siamese. Or maybe he was a blue point. His pedigree was obscured by the fact that he had come to us by casual means. That is, his provenance was questionable and undocumented in any meaningful or official way. I was dealing with problems of provenances in this case, so I looked on the appearance of this animal as something approaching fate. I don't believe in fate. I don't care much for coincidence, either. That's another story.

One of Catherine's students at her school of massage therapy had shown up at class with the creature in her hands. She explained, as Catherine later told me, she'd found the critter huddled in a corner of the school building, behind a scraggly bush where the snow hadn't yet found a deep place. They couldn't keep the thing at the school. Of course not.

Neither the good Samaritan who brought the half-frozen cat inside, nor any of the instructors or students at the school was willing to adopt said feline. The director then stepped in, as she related to me while snuggling very intimately with me in bed that night, and announced that she knew a kind person whom she was sure would take ownership and shelter the animal.

And that's how this unnamed fur ball became part of my household. After three days, living with the creature, it was becoming clear to me and to the two other cats I housed, that our newest boarder was fast becoming the ruler of the palace, regardless of his small stature.

"It's his voice," she whispered. Her pink tongue inserted itself into my ear. Catherine's, not the cat's. "I wonder if it will get any louder,"

I nodded, carefully, so as not to dislodge her sensual ministrations. I loved it when she licked me. Catherine has a well-educated tongue. Living with an accomplished, well-trained massage therapist has its advantages, let me tell you. One of my cats liked to lick me too. Interesting, but nowhere near as sensual. Of course the cats' emotional connection is, I suspect, considerably lower than Catherine's. I certainly hope so.

Yes, it was definitely his voice. As yet unnamed, the fur ball had an intimidating, angry sounding yowl that was as penetrating as anything I had ever experienced out of a Siamese cat. Catherine's strong and agile fingers urged me to roll over and I did. Her tongue continued its ministrations, wandering down my breast bone and across my navel. The cat, apparently sensing complete lack of attention to its yowl remained silent.

* * * *

"You seem to have fallen into a bit of a funk," Catherine said. She was puttering in my kitchen while I stood staring out the deck door at the back yard.

"Have I?"

"Is it the missing woman, or is it the missing book? The one that should have been in the slip case at Gottliebs?"

"Sounds like a line from a song I heard once. I guess my problem is mostly centered around this woman I'm looking for. She seems to have erected an almost impenetrable wall around herself."

"How'd she do that?"

"Usually when that happens successfully, you have someone who lives off the grid, someone who has few legal or social entanglements. In this case, the woman Mr. Gehrz wants found has figured out how to erect such a wall. Or, perhaps, she had some serious technical help. I find her employment, but she doesn't work there anymore and the HR woman I talked to seemed nervous about even telling me that she didn't work there any more.

"I don't mean to suggest a professional hacker couldn't trace her, but I can't. I talked with contacts at the state and mined the little public record available. She has a driver's license and she owns a vehicle. I could get lucky and spot the car while wandering about the city but the chances of that are fairly small, wouldn't you agree?" I grinned at Catherine. "Her address is no longer of this world, being victim of infrastructure rebuilding."

She laughed. I didn't blame her. "Even if you did spot her car on the street, you'd be going the wrong way on a one way street, right?" She laughed again and I smiled with her.

"Can't you get some additional help from your client? Mr. Gehrz?"

"Hah. Mr. Gehrz is a no-show. In spite of several messages I left at the number he gave me, he neither returns my calls nor shows up at my office. I know he's getting my messages, however. I submitted a request for expense reimbursements and lo, there came a wire transfer to my bank from somewhere else."

"Can't you trace that back?"

"Nope. Bank privacy customs deny me access to that information. Now, I suppose I could cultivate somebody at my or some other bank. Somebody who might ultimately be willing to risk their job by feeding me such information."

"The cost-benefit ratio seems out of balance, yes?"

I gave Catherine the eye. She was occasionally wont to spring this CPA-accountant-style language on me. "Yes," I said.

"What next?"

"I shall persevere, plodding on through the highways and byways, the alleys of our metropolis until I find that tiny bit of information that I can exploit. Did I ever mention that I'm pretty good at my job?"

Chapter 10

"Did you get the package?" a woman's voice asked. I instantly recognized the voice. It was my elusive client Anne or Ann, last name unknown, she who was the apparent witness to the murder of a man who may or may not have been Manfred Gottlieb.

"The package? Do I correctly assume it came from you? The package appears to be two pages torn from a book of some kind, possible a ledger. A bound medium-sized ledger, judging by the pages."

I poked the brown wrapping paper with the end of my pencil. It had been heavily taped so I had been forced to cut the tape and wrapping paper to get it open. But I was careful. Always looking for clues.

"Do you read German?"

"No. And why are you sure it's written in German?"

There was a pause and I could hear the woman on the phone breathing rapidly. She sounded agitated. "I haven't seen anything in the paper about progress solving that man's murder."

I was used to clients abruptly changing direction so I trotted right along. "The difficulty is the cops still have no solid connection from what you say you saw on the bridge that night and the body of Mr. Gottlieb. Where did you get these pages?" I was trying to get an admission.

"C'mon, Mr. Sean. What are the chances that whoever I saw thrown off the bridge that night was somebody else? Somebody whose body has totally disappeared?"

She was right, of course. I didn't tell Ann or Anne that there's been no report of anybody else in the city going missing around the time she saw the guy go off the bridge. Fact was, aside from my contact with the cops, and Derrol Madison, Esq., and Aaron Gottlieb, the young man from Chicago, it was shaping up to be an almost perfect crime. Only one anonymous witness, no evidence, no motive. "The other thing is, there's no solid evidence of foul play. For all the authorities can say, Gottlieb fell or jumped."

"But I saw—"

"So you said, but you haven't come forward, have you? You haven't made a statement to the police about what you saw, have you? If you did that, they might take more interest. And another thing. What were you doing on that bridge at that time of night in the middle of a snowstorm? And what's this business of sending me pages torn from a ledger?"

"I told you. I was out walking, something I often do at night."

"So you were apparently within walking distance of your home?" I don't usually do my detecting out loud in front of clients, but I hoped a little provocation might open her up.

"A very tenuous supposition," she retorted.

Again we went silent. I held the phone between my shoulder and ear, cupping the mouthpiece in my left hand. The late morning sun streamed through my office windows. The top of my desk was clear except for the small package and the telephone. I didn't even see any dust.

"I can't come forward, Mr. Sean. I simply can't. I know I should, good citizenship and all that, but it's not in the cards. Not possible. That's why I came to you. I need you to remain as my intermediary, my cut-out, so to say. I have to go now. I'll be in touch."

The call was disconnected before I could even suggest she might soon have to send me more money. I stared at the phone.

Intermediary. Cut-out. She used the words as if they were a normal part of her world. Not everybody did. Odd. Interesting, even.

The telephone rang. Two calls inside one hour. Business was looking up, recession or no.

"Sean Sean, at your service."

Silence. Well, not quite. I could hear breathing.

Then, "Sean, dammit. What are you doing?"

"Excuse me?" There was a crackle and the voice in my ear got wobbly. That often meant a cell phone in motion, like in a car.

"I'm getting inquiries. My staff is asking questions. My partners and associates are talking to possible clients who come in and then disappear. Missed appointments. Wasted time. What the Hell is going on?"

"Madison?" I said. "Is this you?"

"No names," he snapped.

Cloak and dagger shit, I sighed to myself.

"Okay, Sir." I came down hard on the sir. "What is it you want?"

"I want you to make it all go away."

"Let me point out to you the obvious. You have no way of being sure the source of your current agitation has anything to do with me. And if it does, please remember, you came to me, sir. And apart from that meeting and this call we've had almost no contact. I haven't breathed your name to a single soul. If you are feeling exposed, I assume it's either some other client you are involved with, or you were being watched before we met. Is that possible? And here's the biggie, why?"

Silence. Then: "I think the best way to clean this up is to find out what happened to Mr. G. And pronto. That's what I'm paying for."

The connection died. Paying? Madison wasn't paying me anything. He wasn't a client. Or was he? Madison was a good attorney, sharp, always zeroed in on the main points or lapses in the other side's case. But everybody occasionally slips. Even Derrol Madison. Maybe he was paying. Maybe he was fronting for someone. More questions.

I poked at the small brown package. When I'd opened it a few minutes before my client's call, I'd been mildly let down. For some reason that wasn't quite clear to me, the arrival of the small brown package with no return address had seemed to offer some possibilities. An answer or two perhaps.

Inside the brown paper wrapping—metered at a substation on the East Side of Saint Paul, I noted, was an ordinary white business envelope backed by a single piece of blank white cardboard. The envelope wasn't sealed. Inside were two standard white sheets of paper, folded in thirds. On each sheet was a copy of a smaller lined page, apparently, obviously even, torn from a small bound book. Judging from the size of the lined paper, the book was about five inches wide and seven high. The columns printed on the pages looked like what you'd find in a small ledger, the sort one might use to record expenses in. I handled everything gingerly, by the edges, just in case there were fingerprints or DNA. I wasn't holding my breath on that.

On the ledger pages was a series of words, numbers, possibly phrases in some kind of foreign language. It looked to me like a list. The copies weren't numbered so I couldn't tell if the pages were sequential. Did it matter?

I wasn't sure. Ordinarily I might have set the pages aside. What did this have to do with the question of Manny Gottlieb, deceased? I called the Foreign Language Department office at the college in Arden Hills. I didn't want have to deal with parking at the U.

A young sounding woman answered the call. "Here I have a piece of paper for which I need some help in translation. I wondered if there is someone I could meet with today. It's a somewhat urgent matter," I said.

"What's the language?" She queried.

"I don't know for sure but I'm pretty sure it's German. It's hand written."

"Umm. Well, maybe if you spelled out some of the words, I could tell what the language is."

Good idea. So I spelled out several words. *Möbel zwei Bahaus Anrichten.*

"Well," she said after a brief pause, "the second word is two and the third is the name of an artistic movement in Europe in the nineteen twenties. So I'd say it's definitely German, but I don't know the other two words. You know, there are translation programs on the Internet. Are you aware of that?"

I wasn't and said so. She explained that there were programs on the Internet that one could access to translate almost any language into almost any other. "They aren't perfect because regionalisms and dialects can distort subtle meanings, but you can certainly get the gist of your list."

I thanked her and rang off. That's what they say in the UK, I'm told. I think it's a hold-over from the old days when people used real telephone instruments and a bell sounded when you broke the connection.

Never mind. She'd given me an idea. I put the packet into a larger envelope and decamped for home.

When I arrived dark was falling and I found Catherine hard at work on a new lap top computer. I say new because I'd never seen it before, but the thing didn't appear to be brand-spanking new out of the box.

"Whuzzup?"

"After you cautioned me against doing Internet stuff related to your current case on my desktop, I borrowed this machine from my lawyer who swears the protections are so advanced, only NSA or the CIA could ever detect it. This machine is connected to our server through the Wi-Fi link and then only when it's powered up. I just thought you might want some additional research."

"Huh. Thank you, sweetie, that's very thoughtful. What shall we do about dinner?"

"Veal hotdish in the oven. Have a drink. Relax for an hour." She frowned at the big screen inches from her nose. I did as directed and sat beside her.

"I stuck my tongue in her ear which she almost always likes. Then I whispered, "I have need of your assistance. Do you know about on-line translation services?"

"You mean language to language? Sure. They're fairly common." Her fingers flew over the keyboard, pausing only briefly as she followed arcane paths and instructions. "Why do you ask?"

"I have here some pages I want translated."

"Easy. Quickest is to scan them to a flash drive and bring the drive to me."

"Does it matter they are handwritten?"

"Oh. Yes, I'm sure it does. Do you know the language?"

"The script is in German." I held the pages before her. Catherine reached to take them but I whisked them out of range. "Ah, Ah, no touch, please."

Catherine stared intently at me for a moment and then turned her intense gaze back to the pages. For a long moment she eyeballed the page. Then she dipped her eyes to the keyboard and her fingers began to play slowly over the letters. I watched the screen as she connected and called up a translation program. It might have been in Yahoo or Google, I wasn't sure, but then she typed in the same four words I'd given to the woman at the college earlier.

Möbel zwei Bahaus Anrichten. What came back instantly was furniture, two *Bauhaus* sideboards.

I stared at the screen.

"Try this," I muttered. *beschlagnahmen*. I had the word lettered into my notebook and I carefully spelled it out for her.

It came back "cramps." "What the Hell?"

"Wait," Catherine said. She typed some more and this time the English word that came back was "seizures."

We looked at the word. "Oh," Catherine murmured. "Seizures. Not cramps, but as in taking something. Confiscations." We stared at each other for a long silent moment.

Chapter 11

CATHERINE AND I SPEND the better part of the evening, after a sumptuous hotdish of veal and other stuff she had put together, puzzling over the two pages from some mysterious ledger. The writing was small and in places it was smudged as if it had gotten damp. There was almost no punctuation except for a couple of occasional dashes here and there. Mostly what the pages appeared to contain was an inventory of somebody's belongings. Everything, right down to the walls. Not particularly unusual if you were somewhat obsessive about listing possessions.

At Catherine's urging I had such a list of the stuff at my place in Roseville and she maintained one here in Minneapolis. Our lists include some details, where known. Details such as acquisition and purchase price. All useful stuff for insurance purposes, in case of a fire or a bomb. This list appeared to be mostly of items with no particular detail.

There were a few names in the ledger that we recognized, including the afore-mentioned *Bauhaus*. They included a couple of well-known fellows, Raphael and Monet. I assumed these were references to the painters. Catherine wasn't so sure, partly, because we couldn't see any descriptive language. Were these referring to cheap prints? Originals, what? It was as if the writer was deliberately trying to be obscure. *Raphael, X275Y*, was one entry. I began to hope that when I laid hand on the rest of the pages there might be some sort of code or explanation. Always assuming I ever came across the other pages.

The work was complicated. We persisted on into the night, puzzling out the words and then peering at the computer screen. Sometimes the translation programs gave wildly different meanings to the same words. Sometimes the translation changed when a word coupled with other words. It was tedious and I realized, along about the time we started on the second page that if we'd had more context the effort would have been easier.

Bed called and we shut down the computer and toddled off to slumber land. My dreams were easy, that is to say they were nonexistent. At least I didn't remember anything in the morning. My memory loss was helped along by the sight of Catherine's naked form as she sauntered around the bedroom, collecting discarded clothing from the night before.

"I have nothing pressing at school this morning. Do you want to continue translating?"

"I do," I said, "although I suspect we're going to have more of what we've already done. Looks to me like this is just a list of somebody's belongings." I yawned and stretched.

"Possibly, but there might be something in the rest of the page that will offer a clue, give us some context."

"Dim possibility, but it's necessary." I slid out of bed and headed to the shower. When I exited the bathroom Catherine was dressed in her favorite silk shift seated at her computer. The shift showed a lot of very attractive well-toned skin. One glance at her face suggested that she was mentally far away, concentrating on whatever was on the screen. I went to my closet and threw on some clothes. Minutes later I was in the kitchen rustling up some coffee, juice and a cold breakfast of heart-healthy oat cereal. Just a couple of young colts, we were. When the coffee pot signaled done, I yelled down the hall and Catherine appeared.

"Anything of concern? You looked pretty focused there a few minutes ago."

She smiled and drank the orange juice I'd poured. "Nope. Just checking email and reading my DorothyL digest. You're dressed for the world, I see."

"Well, for the office, anyway. No appointments so I'll be making phone calls, trying to locate my two clients of record. They need updates and I need an infusion of cash."

* * * *

THE MAN IN MY OFFICE WAS clearly comfortable with his surroundings, even though I judged he was wearing an expensive tailored suit that put him in a pay grade substantially above mine. His name, he said, was Anderson. He gave off vibes that suggested he was used to more elegant surroundings. It fit him, that dark suit, just like the line on his business card that told me he was an attorney with the Justice Department in Washington. That's D.C. the capitol of the U.S. His card also told me he worked for the Office of Special Investigations. I'd never heard of it before, and I suspect most people haven't either. Mr. Anderson explained tersely that his office focused on tracking down stolen goods from World War Two. He mentioned Simon Wiesenthal.

I had read about Simon Wiesenthal, the famed hunter who dedicated his life to rooting out Nazis who had fled their past associations after the defeat of Nazi Germany in the most recent great war to end all tyranny. Catherine has a book he wrote. Wiesenthal, not this Anderson.

"Mr. Anderson. I don't usually deal with people from the Justice Department. In fact I can't recall the last time it happened. In fact, this is probably a first."

"We had you checked out, Mr. . . . Sean."

"Awkward, isn't it?"

"Excuse me? What is?'

I smiled my disarming smile. It comes naturally so I don't have to practice it. "My names. As you've noticed, they're both the same."

"Yes." Mr. Anderson raised his black eyebrows. "I suppose at times it is a little awkward."

"Right. That's why you paused, just now."

"Mr. Sean, as I started to say, we've had you checked out and almost everything I've learned is positive."

"Thank you. I try." I nodded once. I guess I don't do well with compliments. Catherine mentioned that one time.

"I was in town on agency business and your name came up in connection with this Gottlieb affair."

"Gottlieb affair? I understand there is a dead man in the county morgue with that name attached, but I wasn't aware that it was an affair." I was being cautious. Even overly cautious, perhaps. From the beginning the Gottlieb affair seemed to give off an aura, something slightly unsettling.

"I understand." Anderson steepled his fingers and assumed a thoughtful expression. "However that may be, I wanted you to be aware of your government's interest.

"I don't talk about my cases, even with visiting fe . . . lawyers. Is there something specific I can help you with?"

"Not really. I just wanted to touch base with you and suggest we might be mutually helpful. If you are willing to share what you learn in the course of your investigations, we, your government, would be most grateful. In the spirit of such cooperation, I've called my office to request a search of our files for anything on Mr. Gottlieb we might have that isn't confidential. It's a long shot, but if there's anything useful, I'll see that you receive copies."

"Thanks. Frankly, I'm not sure what useful information the government might have. This seems to be a straight-forward case of a man being murdered, possibly for something he may not even have ever had in his possession."

Raised eyebrows from Mr. Anderson. "I understand. There is another reason I wanted to talk to you. There's a possibility that you might run afoul of some of the fringe element of home grown crazies, like the Aryan Nation, for example. Their potential for violence always seems close to the surface. So, I wanted to express some caution to you. Not a warning, just a heads up."

"I appreciate your concern," I said. "I've been at this business for quite some time and while I've been lucky, I do pay attention to my surroundings."

"Does local law enforcement track hate groups activity?"

"I'm sure they do," I said. "I've never discussed it with my police contacts. I just assume they keep track of such activities." I didn't believe for a nanosecond this guy didn't have the answer to that question.

"You may discover some low-level surveillance, some vandalism, nuisance calls, things like that that haven't happened in the past. If you begin to detect a pattern, don't hesitate to ascribe it to your investigation of Mr. Gottlieb. And be careful." Mr. Anderson smiled a wintry smile while offering this last bit and rising to take up his coat and gloves.

We said a cordial goodbye and he went off. I watched him from my window as he entered the passenger side of a clean dark blue sedan parked at the curb. When it drove off, I could clearly see the government issue license plate. I jotted down the plate number but I knew trying to find out who was driving the vehicle, or what agency it was assigned to would be a monumental waste of time.

* * * *

CATHERINE AND I HAD TALKED about our odd feelings of sometimes being watched. Interestingly it was something we both had recognized in recent days. I had met in an out of the way bar with a lawyer who never said so, but seemed anxious to keep things at arm's length. Derrol Madison was known as a pretty forthright guy so that was odd. I had two other cases with individuals showing greater than normal caution.

Robert Gehrz, the lovelorn lad seeking the missing woman, seemed abnormally skittish. The reticent woman who may have seen the actual murder,

Ann or Anne whatever-her-last-name, was also odd because of the timing. Now I was beginning to wonder if she might be more involved in the Gottlieb incident than I'd been led to believe. I had no particular reason at this time to suspect her of complicity, but people lie to detectives all the time. I expected it. I also expected coincidental events to be almost always resolved with connections when sufficient facts were revealed. More facts, that was the key. I would gird my whatevers and sally forth to do more fact finding, always keeping one eye peeled.

Anne or Ann, she of no last name and uncertain spelling, seemed now in retrospect, to be way too skittish. So did the man I was now calling the Mysterious Mr. Gehrz. They had both paid me a nice chunk of change to do similar tasks. Most of the tasks that came my way were not all that different from these. So why did I have a feeling that Mr. Gehrz and the woman were somehow connected?

I reached into the bottom drawer of my desk and pulled out a well-thumbed copy of *The Concrete Blonde*. Maybe I'd find some answers in its pages.

* * * *

MICHAEL CONNOLLY AND HIS *Concrete Blonde*, while interesting and well-written, was not particularly helpful in my present circumstances. So I went home to our apartment in Kenwood. Since I was early, I was surprised to discover that Catherine had beaten me to it.

"Hey, slack day at the massage parlor?"

"Mmmmm hmmmm."

Her reaction was unusual. Catherine is a bit sensitive to labels attached to her professional career. That's due to the frequent claim that many so-called massage parlors in the city are thinly masked operations of commercial sex. I've never understood why we can commercialize just about everything, but draw the line at sex for hire. But it's not my call is it?

"You are fruitfully engaged I take it?"

"Ummm humm. Make us a drink, please," she responded.

I did that and carried them to the spare bedroom-cum-office where Catherine sat staring intently at her computer screen. I set her drink on the table beside her and glanced at the screen. Then I stared. "Hey! What the Hell is that?"

"Interesting, isn't it?" Nodding enthusiastically. "It looks a lot like the pages you got from that Anne or Ann woman." She took her fingers off the keyboard and picked up her drink.

"For just a second there, I thought it was those pages. What have you got here? Assuming you are going to reveal all."

Catherine sat back. "This morning's paper had a story about a project between the Holocaust Museum and some others to create this database of all the stolen art that's still out there, in the wind as you sometimes characterize it.

"So I went to the site and one of the items was some inventory ledgers from the Bundestag. And when I brought up some sample pages I got these." She gestured at the screen.

"They look nearly identical to the pages we have, don't they?"

She nodded again. "What we have here is pretty conclusive proof that the pages you got are related to the thefts of art and other things in Europe during the Nazi occupation."

"I can buy that, just based on this alone, but let's test the theory some more," I said. "I see some of the pages are typed. Ours are hand-written."

"True, but some of the pages in other books they have are handwritten."

"Style? Handwriting?"

"Not remotely similar," she said sipping her drink. "That doesn't surprise me, Sean."

"Nope. I'd assume whoever was assigned to loot a particular residence, let's say, would make the list in a ledger and then turn the ledger over to some superior officer. Different looting parties had separate ledgers."

"In the case of Parisian looting, the superior officer would be Reichsleiter Alfred Rosenberg. He was in charge there."

"Any references to the area of Poland where Gottliebs came from?"

"None that I can find. I think this is confined to Central Europe. The inventories on the website are labeled unidentified Jewish owners."

"They are samples, I suspect. Those that have been specifically identified are probably being handled with more delicacy," I said.

"There are date stamps from 1943," Catherine said. She shut down the computer and we ambled to the kitchen to prepare supper.

"I need to get that woman to send me more of the ledger pages," I said. At the moment, I had no idea how dangerous and complicated that would become.

Chapter 12

THE TRUCK CAME OUT of nowhere. Not entirely true, of course. It came from somewhere, mostly out of the dark alley on my left. And it went somewhere. I couldn't say where. I was head over tea kettle in a dirty snow bank. The one thrown up by a city plow trying to stay ahead of what seemed this winter to be constant snow falls. That's why I didn't see where the damn truck went.

I had been trudging through the cold afternoon twilight toward a small bar on the north side of downtown, not far from the new Target Center, which was near the newer Target Twins Baseball field which was quite close to . . . well, you get the idea. I had my head down, never a good idea for a private detective, whether on a case or not, and I definitely was on a case. It came close to being Sean's last case. I was trudging along when this small box truck blasted out of the alley. Fortunately my reflexes are still pretty good, and I flung myself backward and to the right. So I ended up in this snow bank, as I said. I suppose it was fortunate that there was so much snow that season so there was a large relatively soft snow bank close at hand.

I remember thinking that red Keds were not exactly appropriate footwear, and my feet were getting chilled. The truck roared at me, blaring its horn as an afterthought and then sliding into the street and out of sight around the next corner. Now this could have been one of those random accidents that occur in the big city. You know, small insignificant person (myself) unfortunately run down and crushed by inattentive driver of commercial vehicle. Except that the truck kept going in a great hurry and flurry of snow and slush. Except it didn't have its lights on and the driver didn't blow his horn first. I conclude from all that, plus other odd events in my recent life, that this was an attempt to take me out of the picture. Or the action.

I gathered from that that I must be getting somewhere in my unending quest for answers to the important questions of my time. You know, questions like, where is Robert Gehrz, who is Anne or Ann and why are people paying attention to this humble private investigator who seeks merely to serve his clients? I regained my feet, brushed myself off while hurling some meaty and obscene imprecations at the departing driver. Well, the Justice Department lawyer had warned me, hadn't he? He'd told me that when private citizens get involved, things can get messy. And dangerous. By this time, I was convinced somebody was out to dust me, put out my lights, cancel my reservation. It was adding measurably to my irritation. Unlike some cases, I couldn't just chuck it. I had no way to terminate—bad choice of words I guess—my relationship with Mr. Gehrz because he wasn't anywhere in evidence. He'd left my office telling me he'd be in touch if I needed more gelt, but that had apparently been a small lie. Aaron Gottlieb, on the other hand was all over my case. Even though he'd gone back to his life in Chicago and wasn't due to return to Minneapolis unless and until there were significant developments, he called almost every day with a question or a thought.

So I bounced up, brushed myself off and continued on my lonely way to the bar. It's called Casey's, should anyone ask. It's a blues bar. That is because, on most evenings a solo guitarist, occasionally a keyboardist, would appear on the postage-stamp-sized stage at the back corner of the place and entertain the local patrons with some down-and-sad soulful music. Sometimes the music was slow and dark, other times it might leach a little more into modern rhythms. Blues music is a label not given to precise definitions. It bears some similarities to crime or mystery fiction in that regard. Tonight the performer was a man I happen to know.

Michael Katz was a classically trained harpsichordist, keyboardist, guitarist, and he had a nice singing voice in the bargain. A long time ago he'd aborted a career with a rock band in another city at the dawn of the rock-and-roll era for greater stability with an academic life. But the call of the music is sometimes hard to resist. So here we were, and because of his ethnicity, it occurred to me that he might be a useful source of background information. I didn't expect he ever knew the dead Gottlieb, but he might very well have known of people with the kind of background and experience similar if not identical to Mr. Gottlieb's. The kind of experience that gets you killed.

I warmed myself in the noisy, convivial atmosphere of Casey's blues bar and listened to the music. When Katz took a break he was doing a solo gig tonight, I offered to buy him a drink, which he accepted.

"Nice to see you here," he said, "but I suspect you aren't merely on the town for a little culture."

"And how do you deduce that, my friend?"

"You're alone. Your tall and lissome friend isn't with you."

"Astute observation."

"Well, my Ph.D. is good for something. You're never or almost never seen as a couple when you're working so I assume your dropping in is not a casual occurrence."

Since Katz was right, I explained some of what I needed to know. I was careful to avoid entangling my acquaintances and friends in my cases in any way other than the most peripheral, so telling all was not on the table.

"Why do you have dirty snow melting on your shoulders?"

Katz had interrupted my thought and I looked at him with my mouth hanging open. "Excuse me?"

"Not that I consider you a sartorial icon, but I wonder if you've been burrowing in snow banks."

I explained about my truck-dodging incident.

"You need to acquire a body guard who could punch out the truck motor, like Bubba? That friend of Kenzie and Gennaro?"

"What I'd like to learn," I said, after the woman who served as waitress and often bartender at the same time, refreshed my weak drink and slunk back down the bar. "What I'm wondering is this. I've learned that the invaders who overran Europe in the previous century and looted thousands of privately and publically held art works, frequently kept meticulous and detailed records of their depredations."

Michael Katz nodded. "This is true."

"In the aftermath of the war, some G.I.s brought home a little loot from the war. I guess that happened a good deal. You would agree?"

"Sure. What I've read is that most of the booty soldiers carried home in their duffels were weapons and medals and flags, stuff like that. And art."

"Art," I said.

"Yeah. Lost art from the big war is something that has interested me. Parenthetically, did you know the Nazis also looted whole houses of furniture and other stuff. They stripped homes to the walls."

"What happened to all that?"

"A lot was destroyed during the war, some was put into use elsewhere in Europe and some is still missing."

I sucked on an ice cube. I normally don't take ice in my scotch, but I hadn't been paying close attention when the bartender came by the last time with a new drink. This one was stronger than the last.

"Did you know," Katz continued, "that there are an estimated ten thousand plus pieces of art still unaccounted for? Some of it quite valuable."

"Wow."

"Wow indeed."

"How do you know this?" I asked.

"Records. Like you just said, those Nazis, in addition to all the horrendous things they did to people, kept records of their thefts and other stuff. There are records of the numbers of people murdered in the death camps. They even kept track of the numbers of shoes and more ghoulish things that resulted from the wholesale slaughter. Some Nazis forced Jews to sign faked bills of sale so they could later claim legitimate purchases."

Michael's voice quavered with rage and he stopped to take a long breath.

"Sorry," he said and went on in a more normal tone. "Many of the records are lost, of course, but most were found and are still being mined for evidence. People are spending their entire careers trying to locate objects that belonged to their ancestors."

"And you know about this how?"

"A distant cousin is one of those seekers," Katz nodded solemnly. "I've never met the man but we correspond occasionally. He reads and speaks English, but I have to have his letters translated when he writes to me."

"All right. So let me ask you this. If some GI returned home to Minneapolis, say with a valuable jewel or a painting, for example, would that be worth dying over?"

Katz frowned. "I shouldn't think so, not all by itself. But the circumstances might suggest something different." I was watching his face and I saw that in his mind he went away from Casey's blues bar for a moment.

After a minute or so I said, "Let me give you a scenario. Suppose a man brings home a small painting. Years later somebody discovers he has it, wants it back and murders the guy to get it. Make any sense?" I asked.

"No, especially since nearly all the people directly involved are either dead or almost so. But think about alternatives. What else, other than a jewel or some other artifact, might a soldier bring home? And consider the effects of what came home. A lot of relatively worthless souvenirs. But maybe something of real value?" He stopped and I thought he was going to continue in that vein. But then, "I have to go back to work." Katz stood and extended his hand. "Intriguing questions, my friend. Let me know how it all turns out." I watched him mount the small stage and thought about what I had just learned.

Chapter 13

I STILL WASN'T SURE WHAT I had learned from my guitar-playing friend, but there was this feeling. It's something that happens to me periodically during a case. It's a sense that I'm getting somewhere, although the where may not yet be entirely clear. In other words, I was becoming the repository of almost a sufficient number of facts to solve the puzzle. Or at least part of the puzzle. I just had to sort and resort until links appeared and facts became associated with other facts. In this case, one of the problems was that I still couldn't see the outline of the whole puzzle. Having the edges of a jigsaw in place frequently made the whole easier to solve.

Meanwhile, back at the ranch, storm clouds appeared on the horizon. Not real ones, of course.

"I haven't made as much progress as I think I should by this time."

Catherine glanced up from her busy fingers preparing what looked like a fine green salad at the kitchen counter. "I'm sorry to hear that. Can I help?"

"You might do a computer search for me. Look up the family Gottlieb." I thought about what I was asking. "Only it might be better if you did it from a public computer, since you returned the loaner."

Catherine's busy fingers paused. "I've added a program. It conceals my digital footprints from all but the most sophisticated mining programs."

"Really? You can do that?" I sauntered to the refrigerator and found some ice cubes in the freezer section. "Since when? And what are mining programs?"

She explained that programmers have figured out how to keep track of which sites Internet users go to, the better to target advertising. "Other programmers are just as quickly figuring out how to shield Internet users against such tracking. We now have such a shield." She grinned and reached for the drink I had just made for her. "Now I update it every year. I get a little help from my friendly tech."

"I'll be damned." I knew Catherine had computer skills far superior to mine, which are at the unsophisticated toddler level. I mean, I can turn the thing on and off and type stuff that manages to stick around. "Apparently you knew, even before I did that I might have to ask for technical help from time to time."

"Sure. And when I thought about the kind of profession you're in, it occurred to me that leaving a trail back to Lucy," she nodded toward our office, "would be unwise. Thanks for the drink."

I smiled up at my companion. "My pleasure. You have some amazing connections." Catherine also had a habit of naming some of her belongings. Her computer was Lucy, her favorite massage table is Max and her new BMW is as yet nameless. Having examined Max intimately on more than one occasion, I was as yet unable to determine how Max differed from other massage tables, but it wasn't something I worried about. "So Lucy has a digital veil over her trail, is that it?"

"Yep. I'm sure the NSA could penetrate it but why would they? It's something I think you ought to consider for that ancient monstrosity in your office. If such protection is even available for a machine that old. Maybe I'll gift you a slick new PC or Apple for some holiday or other. Your birthday?" She slid the salad bowl aside and turned to examine the plastic-wrapped porterhouse steak thawing in a bowl of warm water.

The ancient monstrosity in my office she referred to was my four-year-old Dell PC. "I almost never use the Internet connection you insist I have installed. Email is one of the biggest wastes of time ever invented. Worse than the plague," I grumbled.

"Wait until I get you hooked up with Facebook and Twitter," she smirked. She picked up the floating steak and poked it. "I think it's about ready for the broiler." The way she poked and caressed the steak with her talented fingers reminded me of her expertise at massage, a skill I was happy to indulge at every opportunity.

Two culinary techniques I'd introduced to Catherine were brining fowl carcasses and bringing steak, beef in particular, to room temperature before grilling. Especially on the barbecue. It was entirely too cold this February day to grill on our miniscule deck, but we had this indoor grill device. A George Herman, or something. I don't know what I think about naming cooking utensils after human beings. It isn't the same, of course, this indoor grill in a metal "fence," but it's still pretty good. If you bring a steak to room temperature before you grill, you get better charring and more even cooking all the way through, whatever your desired level of doneness happens to be.

After dinner we relaxed with a fine brandy. "I'm starting to hear things," Catherine said.

"You're hearing things?"

"Umm, about you."

I sat up. I didn't like that. I'm not one of those high profile P.I.s or lawyers you hear about on TV or read about in the newspapers. That's not my thing. Quiet and self-effacing is more my style. After more than twenty years of P.I.-ing, I can walk into almost any law office or corporate HQ or small shop on the street and go unremarked as a complete, if shorter than average, stranger. With the exception of the cops I know and my street contacts, I'm nobody. I like it that way. The closest to public exposure I ever get in the local daily is "an unnamed source is reported to have said . . ." So when Catherine says she's hearing things about me, I have to pay attention.

"I teach an adult class at Beth-El."

"Yes."

"The other day I heard two of my students talking about something the rabbi said. It had to do with local efforts to trace some stolen art."

"Was my name mentioned?"

"No. Apparently there is a private organization called Atria. It specializes in trying to trace art that was stolen by the Nazis in World War Two, and where it may have ended up. The art."

"Atria, as in atrial, something about the heart." I thought a moment. "Isn't an atrium the Roman singular for atria? An open space surrounded by a structure, like a residence courtyard or something?"

Catherine nodded. "I think that's right. Anyway, the student said the rabbi said she'd had an inquiry from a local Atria representative. Then the two students speculated about that. They seemed to know what the name represented."

"Interesting, but I don't see a link to my own self."

"Ah, wait. I'm getting to that."

I twisted on the couch so I could look into Catherine's face. She didn't look anything but relaxed, maybe a tad solemn, perhaps.

"For no apparent reason that I can explain, later at the office I did an Internet search. There really isn't anything to find that seemed relevant except one entry. Atria in Minneapolis. No address just a phone number. So I called it. Whoever answered said I'd reached the law offices of Derrol Madison."

I sat up suddenly. Derrol Madison, the powerful, wheel-chair-bound, attorney. Derrol Madison who had met with me in an out-of-the-way restaurant to enlist my help with a non-client from Chicago named Aaron Gottlieb. A non-client of his, attorney Madison was careful to point out. Madison had shrugged off my question about how this grand nephew of the murdered Gottlieb had located and contacted Mr. Attorney Derrol Madison.

"And that's how my name came up?"

"I mis-spoke. What I should have said was that I'm hearing gossip about this case you're involved in. The Gottlieb affair."

There was that word again. Affair. I was beginning to think a simple murder investigation had morphed into an international spy game. I don't have the resources to compete with spies and terrorists. They are like the mob. Too much money and a level of ruthlessness I'm not up for.

Some time later, after we'd gone to bed and all that implies, I abruptly awoke and sat up. I stared into the darkness at the pale rectangle of window. Beside me, I listened to Catherine's even breathing. I could tell she wasn't fully asleep. After a moment, her drowsy voice said, "Something bothering you?'

"Yeah, there is. It's a link, a connection that I can't quite grab hold of. It's something floating out there just beyond me. Thing is, it feels alarming, as if I ought to know or do something to avoid a big pothole in the highway. I think it would be a really good idea if you happen to do any Internet stuff for me in the next few weeks, for you not to use your computers at school. In fact I'm not even sure about Lucy."

Chapter 14

The new February morning had dawned like most of them so far this year. Dark, dreary, overcast with low heavy clouds. A wind was blowing down all the city canyons. Was it a raw wind? I had no way of knowing, but it made things even more miserable.

I was in my office when the door opened and this tall, good-looking, blond sashayed in. No, that's a line from one of Chandler's books, I think. The door did open but a man of small stature stepped in. It was my landlord. He smiled and said, "We're redoing the office down the hall for a new tenant. It'll be a little noisy at times. Just wanted you to know."

I smiled and nodded.

He nodded back and went out, closing the door softly behind him.

I went back to my puzzle. I had laid out some note cards like the ones you used to find in the library card catalogue. I printed a brief note on each, like the name of one of the players. Gehrz, for example and his apparent job. A Gottlieb, nephew, Man. Gottlieb, doa. Ann/Anne—NLN, missing. For some of them the notes were more extensive. I had decided on my way to the office that my paying client, Gehrz, should be part of this exercise. After all, I had no reason to exclude him.

I threw in a cop for the hell of it, Ricardo Simon, my homicide buddy. He hadn't caught the death of Manny Gottlieb, but the department wasn't that big that cases weren't shared. He might tell me a few things. If I asked the right questions. But what did I know?

M. Gottlieb died presumably protecting something, some physical object. Two men murdered him. A woman, Ann/Anne NLN hires yours truly to find evidence to put the two men away. I have a card with Anne and two large black question marks on it.

A guy named, he says, Robert Gehrz, shows up and hires me to *cherchez la femme*. The *femme* in question is a woman he's been dating who seems to have disappeared. I take the case knowing this is such a wildly improbable scenario as to strain credulity. But the money is nice, and I can always be a cut out if it appears said female doesn't want to be found—after I locate her.

Of course.

Next a card for Derrol Madison, attorney at law. He meets me in a small out of the way bar to ask me to meet and help Aaron Gottlieb, grand nephew of the dead guy. From Chicago. I do and have another client. Another card. It's beginning to remind me of that good novel I just read, *Too Many Clients*, by David Walker.

Then there is the house and the tenant, Ursula Skranslund, Finnish graduate student. Another file card. I decide to make two cards, one for the student and another for the house itself.

I wasn't making significant progress finding the woman Gehrz wanted me to locate, and I wasn't aware of the cops making much progress finding the killer or killers of Manny Gottlieb. So I made another card, this one for a group named Atria.

According to Ann/Anne, the two who threw Manny off the bridge were after something he wouldn't or couldn't give them. So I made a card for an object. I labeled it the Maguffin.

Then I realized what my subconscious mind had done. It's probably the same hook my head was wrestling with last night in bed. Many clients, one case. Perhaps. Self, I ask, let me pose this supposition.

Suppose the woman who saw the murder of Gottlieb is the same woman that slick Mr. Gehrz is looking for? And suppose Anne/Ann was in position to witness the murder because she is somehow connected to both Gottlieb and the Maguffin. If Slick Gehrz is looking for Anne/Ann, then it stands to reason he too is looking for the Maguffin.

Let us not forget the truck that tried to kill me. Another card, although I don't usually make cards for incidents. Then there was the guy from Justice. Not a client, but somebody who has an interest in this puzzle. So I made a card for the U.S. Justice Department, Office of Special Services.

I went downstairs to the tiny sandwich place in the lobby and got me a ham and cheese on rye. When I got back upstairs to my office, the telephone was ringing, so I answered it.

"You're in the mud again," said Detective Ricardo Simon when I picked up.

"What? Why?"

"Manny Gottlieb? There's a fire at his house."

"Oh, shit."

"Indeed. Thought you ought to know. Why do so many of your cases seem to have complications for us?"

He hung up and I wondered about Ursula Skranslund while I grabbed coat and cap and gloves and charged out of the office. I nearly bowled over a workman carrying a short stepladder down the hall toward the site of the renovations. By the time I got to my car and skidded into Central Avenue, reason suggested that, since I wasn't a fireman and the City of Minneapolis had a professional firefighting operation, there wasn't going to be anything for me to do there except observe.

So instead of tearing dangerously along icy streets, running red lights and endangering myself and half the city's pedestrians, I took twenty minutes to reach the scene.

There wasn't much to see. By that I mean, nothing much out of the ordinary. Smoke billowed out of the attic windows. Firemen secured to the slippery inclines by safety ropes went about their tasks, chopping vent holes in the roof. Other fire people—impossible to tell men from women—hauled and aimed hoses that squirted tons of water into the upper floors, water that then ran down the walls and seeped into cracks and crevices. The water would stagnate and breed mold and creepy crawlies. The place would be unlivable at least for months, if it ever could be lived in again.

I found a battalion commander by his red automobile just outside the perimeter established by the trucks. He shook his head when I ambled up.

"Shame. These old houses ought to better protected."

I introduced myself. "I've met the woman renting a room there."

"You know the owner?"

I nodded and did a bad imitation of a turtle to try to protect the back of my neck from the winter wind. "His name is Aaron Gottlieb. He lives in Chicago. He's related to the previous owner, recently deceased." The fire guy frowned as if the name had some meaning for him. "Did I recently read about a Gottlieb found dead on the river ice?"

"The same. He was the home owner. It's probable the guy was murdered." I didn't want to be too forthcoming with the commander, possibly prejudice his attitude.

"Murdered. Huh." He fished a cell phone out of his jacket and dialed a number. I stepped away to give him some privacy. The conversation was brief, but the man's attention to me had clearly sharpened. "So, Mr. Sean, you have anything to tell me?"

"More questions than anything." I proceeded to tell him what I recalled and gave him particulars on how to reach Ursula Skranslund at her new place somewhere in southeast. "I assume there's no body?"

"That's right. There's something a little odd about this fire." He paused. His stare was cool.

"Such as?" I filled the empty air to hurry things along. My feet were beginning to grow numb.

"The fire apparently started in the attic."

"Odd is it? Near a large upright storage cabinet?"

"That's it. Just preliminary observations, of course, but attic fires in older well-maintained homes like this one are a little unusual."

"Odd, you said."

"Yes."

"Perhaps you will look for an accelerant of some kind."

"You can count on it."

"May I call you later on for an update as the investigation proceeds?"

The commander smiled at my choice of language. "I'd consider it a privilege to share information. Nice meeting you, Mr. Sean." We exchanged business cards. I'd recently started carrying cards Catherine had had produced for me.

I went away from the stink of charred wood and the noise of large diesel engines, the shouts of men carrying ice-encrusted hoses. I went back to my office and my growing pile of little white file cards. The day continued dark and dreary.

Chapter 15

"Your phone is compromised."

I recognized the voice immediately, although we rarely spoke together.

"Mr. Madison. What do you mean, my phone is compromised?"

"I had a technician sweep your offices and your connections. He says you need to upgrade and buy some shields. Never mind that. You are clean at the moment but I don't know when they'll reinstall a tap."

"Who's this 'they?'"

Madison ignored my question. "That establishment where we met the first time?"

"Up north? Yeah, I remember. What time?"

"Four this afternoon work for you?"

I checked my pocket calendar and nodded at the phone. "Sure," I said. "See you then."

My phone was compromised? What a thing to say. How did he know that? Was it even true? I was liking this whole business less and less.

I was late to our rendezvous. A snow squall that blew across the northern suburbs jammed up traffic considerably. Madison was ensconced in his wheelchair at a table with his back to the outside wall near one corner of the place. He had a drink in front of him. He wasn't easy to spot unless you were looking for him as I was. Madison had placed himself so he could see the whole room and anybody coming or going from the two exits.

I stopped at the bar for a scotch and water and took it to the table. They didn't stock Macallan so I settled for the bar scotch. I sat with my back to the room. No itchy feeling crawled up between my shoulder blades, even though I was reminded of scenes in some western movies.

"Well, here I am," I said. "Sorry for being late. Traffic is a mess."

"I almost gave up on you," he said, looking at me over the rim of his glass.

"What gives? And what's with that crack about my phone being bugged?"

Madison sipped what looked like a whiskey sour and said, "You've apparently stumbled onto one of my projects. I prefer to keep my involvement with Atria below the radar where possible."

"Does this have something to do with Aaron and Manny Gottlieb?"

Madison nodded and took another drink. I didn't know him well, never socialized with him, so it was hard to read him. But he seemed off, a little nervous. He put his glass down and rotated it between his fingers.

"Yes, it does. In a way. First, I need to give you some background. About Atria."

I nodded encouragingly. At least I thought so.

"Atria is a loose organization of people who are interested in European history. Specifically they—we—do research into the aftermath of World War Two. It's not a tightly organized group because we try to maintain a low profile. The local Atria is not very large. There are similar organizations around the world, and we have links with most of them."

"Okay," I said. The scotch slid nicely down my throat.

"We get information in a variety of ways, much of it word of mouth. Most of it incomplete."

"So a lot of what you acquire is unverifiable? Gossip? Water cooler stuff?"

"Exactly. Somebody gives us a letter, or a fragment of a letter, maybe an old blurry photograph of somebody who looks like somebody. We also get depositions. Most of those depositions are from older individuals who want some kind of justice. They want the people responsible to pay."

"We're talking about specific accusations of wrongdoing, right?" I said.

"That's correct," Madison nodded. "Here's an example of what I mean." He took another drink. I could see he was warming to his subject. "I got a call a couple of days ago from an old woman." He shrugged. "At least she sounded old. She wouldn't give me her name. She said she was at the Mall of America with her granddaughter the other day. She refused to say what day or how long ago. She said she saw a man she recognized from the old country."

"And I bet you asked what country and she wouldn't tell you, right?"

Madison nodded. "Then she told me the name she knew him by in the camp where she was held during the war."

He didn't have to tell me what war he was talking about.

"Now this woman must be in her eighties or nineties and her eyesight is maybe not so good any more. Maybe her memory is also faulty. I don't know because I've never met her. She read me the number she said was tattooed on her forearm. And she said the man's name and that he'd been a guard or trustee at her camp. Her concentration camp."

"Did his name mean anything to you? Did you recognize it?"

Madison nodded again. "Yes, but not the way you mean."

I raised one eyebrow.

"The name she used is a prominent political family in Minnesota." He stopped and licked his lips. It was almost as if he was afraid to say it aloud. "Murchison."

I raised both eyebrows.

"Exactly my reaction," Madison said in a lower tone. "Not possible. She's mistaken. Plus, when I checked, we found no record of a guard or trustee with that name at that camp. What's more, as far as we could determine, everybody in that camp's administration is dead. Still, she could be right and the records are wrong or incomplete.

"So who did she see or think she saw? We have no clue except, guess what? Research into the Murchison family tree reveals that a branch of the family with an almost identical name came from that part of Europe. I'm telling you this so you understand what Atria is and what it does and doesn't do. A lot of the bits and pieces we get can only be classified as gossip, gossip that would be slanderous and even libelous if some kind of action ensued without incontrovertible proof. Documentation. This is all fragmented and very difficult. We aren't interested in stirring things up unnecessarily or making nebulous accusations."

I love listening to lawyer talk. Sometimes. "I get it. Atria collects all this stuff and looks into it as time and resources permit, right? And most of it just gets filed away because no corroborating evidence shows up. Or it gets filed until some other fragment appears. Am I correct?"

"You are. But there are the exceptions. Sometimes we get a name or a query from somebody that links to information in our files or from another organization that has sent us a query. And then there are possible links to missing art, to missing belongings of various kinds. The Nazis confiscated all kinds of stuff, a lot of which has been deliberately destroyed or is missing."

"Ah," I said. "That's a particularly thorny issue, I take it."

"The amount of money potentially involved is huge. Let me give you a hypothetical. I'll say that you are living and working in Germany in 1940.

You have money, and over months and years you've acquired a number of paintings by the Austrian painter, Gustav Klimt. Comes a knock on the door and a band of thugs roars through your house and confiscates a couple dozen of your paintings, knocking you on your ass in the bargain. Today, you're dead, your immediate family is likewise, but some of your descendants are alive and those heirs believe they have some rights to those paintings. You follow?"

"Sure. After the war lots of stuff was recovered, there were hundreds, maybe thousands of art pieces, still unrecovered."

"Some of them," Madison continued, "were sold, some are in museums or private hands with faulty provenances, and most of them are worth significant money."

"Define significant," I asked.

"The Klimt collection? Upwards of two hundred million U.S." Madison swallowed the last of his drink.

"Dollars? You're exaggerating," I said, staring across the table at the lawyer. To say I was startled would understate the case. A short unremarked private investigator living in the Upper Midwest rarely if ever comes into contact with such wealth. Particularly in the world of high art and culture.

"Probably more by now. Well, last year, an old Polish fellow showed up in my office. He asked for a representative of Atria. That's unusual. Most of my office people don't know about Atria, much less my connection. I met with the man and he explained that he believed he had stumbled across a connection to somebody in Minneapolis who was somehow involved in prison camps during the 1940s. Maybe the man was a murderer," he said.

"He went on to state he might have evidence that somebody in town was profiting from events at one of the concentration camps active during World War Two. He further stated that his family home had been looted when they were sent off to the camp and he produced a list of their possessions."

Madison reached into his inside pocket and brought out an envelope. He fished out a single sheet of paper and unfolded it. When he did so, I recognized it. It was a copy, very much like two I already had, of a page from a small ledger that was once enclosed in a slipcase labeled "Seizures."

"Manfred Gottlieb," I said, staring down at the sheet of paper.

"Manfred Gottlieb," echoed Madison.

Chapter 16

I looked at the piece of paper Madison had placed on the table between us. Then I looked at Madison. "Why do I get the feeling we're dealing with dynamite here?"

He didn't smile. "Because we are. Mr. Gottlieb accused a family well-known in the Twin Cities of being connected to those long ago events. The Murchisons."

"But—"

Madison raised one long finger, a move I'd seen him use in court. "And this is why we move so slowly and cautiously. Even one incorrect accusation like this can be disastrous to our work. Obviously, it's highly unlikely that the man accused is still alive. But his family is and we're not about to sully their reputations plural, without incontrovertible proof."

"This page here is not proof," I murmured. We'd both lowered our voices even though there was no one sitting near our table.

"Not by itself. If there were more pages, it would help. If we had the rest of the pages from what appears to be a ledger, that would help. Frankly, even with the whole ledger, assuming that it's similar to those we know about, we might not have enough to actually accuse someone. The information could lead to some restitutions, however."

"Okay, I understand. The thing is, I'm really not interested in going after the descendents of whoever this is. They can't be held responsible for acts committed before they were born, can they?"

Madison shook his head. "I agree with you, except for one thing. This particular family, assuming again that Gottlieb's information is correct, appears to have directly profited from those crimes."

"Ah, I see."

"Ah, indeed," said Madison. "Atria is following up on some additional leads, but I'm not very hopeful. I had the impression that Mr. Gottlieb had the rest of the ledger or at least more pages. But he wouldn't say and he refused to tell or show me anything more without something in return."

"Like what?"

Madison stared at me. "We didn't get to that."

I stared at the wall behind Madison's head. Then I told him what the woman Anne/Ann had described to me, how Mr. Gottlieb had wound up dead on the river ice. "That suggests to me that someone in this town is anxious to lay hands on and probably destroy the ledger."

"Watch your back, Sean." We shook hands and Madison wheeled himself out of the bar. I presumed he had someone to help him or he would have asked. I finished my Scotch, went into the darkening afternoon, and drove back to my office.

Unlike many of my cases, the more I learned about the Gottlieb murder, and I had almost no doubt now that the woman Ann/Anne was telling me the truth about what she'd observed, the more certain I was that I was in imminent danger of getting in over my head.

Back to my growing pile of index cards. An hour later, getting near supper time, it was dark, of course. Somebody once remarked that we P.I.s do our best work in the dark of the night. P.I.s and vampires. When somebody banged on my door, I slid open the lower left drawer where I sometimes keep a small gat. My friend, detective Ricardo Simon, made me remove the revolver I had affixed to the underside of the lap drawer, demonstrating that I could inadvertently plug somebody, which would be very bad for business. Besides, the landlord had insisted I unfasten the guest chair from where I'd screwed it to the floor.

"Come," I hollered when my visitor rapped again. The door opened and a man I didn't know entered. He was bundled up against the cold and he was carrying a tool box.

"I'm Jesse Toogood," he said.

"Okay," I ventured.

"From Electronics R Us? You wanted a sweep?"

"Sure." I waved him in. Madison had told me my phone was bugged. Later at the bar he'd admitted he had no evidence but he wanted to get my attention. So I'd called my friendly IT tech who worked for a well-known technical squad who specialized in Internet and computer installations and repair. ERU was a moonlight operation I used occasionally for bugging and other electronic surveillance, things not strictly legal. So it followed they could purify my office if indeed Madison was right about a bug.

"I was here earlier, but you were all locked up."

"Business. You got ID?" He was already fishing a card case out of his inside pocket. It was the same move a killer going for a shoulder holster would make. His business card had an odd blue squiggle in one corner that I recognized. To the casual observer it looked like he'd nicked the corner of the card with a ball point pen. To those few who knew, it was a mark that legitimized the carrier.

"Make yourself at home. Just the one room is all I have."

Mr. Toogood dropped his big puffy coat on my guest chair and unpacked the tool box. He hooked a wand on a cable to a black box. Then he systematically went over my office from top to bottom, side to side and paid particular attention to the electronics on my desk.

After twenty minutes he shrugged and said, "Nothing here. You're clean as a new cue ball."

I thanked him, and Jesse Toogood packed up, dressed up and disappeared. I called Catherine and told her I was going home to Roseville tonight. The cats needed tending and I didn't like leaving the house unvisited too many winter nights in a row.

The drive home was uneventful, no vehicle appeared to be following me. No shots were fired in my immediate vicinity. My service had plowed out the driveway and the motion-sensitive perimeter light fixtures dutifully flashed on when I entered the driveway. I could tell the temperature was dropping. A few flakes of white stuff drifted down. I stuck out my tongue and tasted the cold icy snow as I put the key in the door and went into a warm house.

My two-cat greeting committee was impatiently waiting at the door. They complained that I had been neglecting them in favor of more human contacts but that could have just been my impression. I don't speak cat. For penance I opened a fresh can of high-end cat food and gave them each a couple of morsels. They wolfed down the treats with hardly a pause, as though they figured their next meal would be a long time coming. The back-up supply of bowls of dry food were not quite empty.

Moving into the kitchen I found a bottle of twelve-year-old Macallan and poured myself a drink. The good scotch went down smoothly, and I turned to the small pile of mail that had accumulated in my absence. I set aside two bills and went through city notices and several ads. After a quick scan of each, that all went into the recycle bin. I almost always scan the ads sent to me. One sometimes learns odd bits, such as a late night fast food restaurant changing its hours. Late night hunger sometimes comes with my business.

I wrote checks from my household account for the two bills. Yes, I know there are electronic and automatic payment systems, but I like writing checks. It keeps me in touch with my money. Real money in and out, bank statements. It's too easy to forget that income and outgo have real consequences with all the automation that pervades our lives. Just tap a few buttons. One day the process servers show up, the water and electricity are turned off and foreclosure happens. By then it's a few dollars too late. Roseville streets are cold and inhospitable in the winter.

I fired up my home computer and discovered I was overdue to change the furnace air filter. While I did that, a scenario built in my mind. Manny Gottlieb was trudging across the Stone Arch Bridge on that recent February night. Nobody had yet figured out why he was there in that snowstorm. He went over the railing, helped by two men, according to the mysterious Anne/Ann. Apparently the two murderers had been following Gottlieb. But why was the woman out there? Sure, she said she often took that walk late at night. But that night it was cold and storming, a near blizzard. What a coincidence!

Baloney. My BS meter told me she was there because she was either following the two guys or she was following Gottlieb. That meant she must be involved at some other level. Of course, she could have been the one who levered Mr. Gottlieb over the rail and onto the river ice, but my instincts said no. I thought she presented the scene just as it happened, except for the things she was apparently leaving out. I thought the omissions might contain vital keys to a solution. I was going to have to look more intensely at this woman. Links. Circles within circles. Nevertheless, not to be forgotten was the lonesome fact that I only had her word and my gut for what had gone down out there on the bridge. That and the deceased Mr. Gottlieb.

I finished changing the furnace filter and went upstairs to fry me a chunk of beef. Twice in one week. I had to watch my diet.

As long as I was dancing along lines of speculation, suppose Ann/Anne was in that place because she was following Mr. Gottlieb and maybe she was doing that because she hoped he'd lead her to whatever she was looking for. Now, if that was the case she could be some kind of agent, and it would make sense she wanted the murderers caught, but couldn't be publically linked to the event. It would blow her cover, so to speak.

My life was definitely becoming more complicated.

Chapter 17

THE NOTE BROUGHT ME OUT very late that night and I wasn't happy. Snow, large, blobby flakes of the stuff were drifting down. I could see them in the glow of distant street lights. My breath was a pillow-cloud of moisture that bloomed and then wandered off. The snow seemed to muffle the sounds of the sleeping city that lay all around. It would have been romantic if it wasn't so freakin' cold. The texture of the scene was also altered by my knowledge that the man standing in the narrow doorway behind me had one hand under the unzipped side of his thick jacket so his standard issue Glock was in easy reach of his fingers. Off-duty Detective Sergeant Ricardo Simon shuffled his galoshes-clad feet, making a soft shushing noise.

I wanted to swing my hands together in a heavy clapping motion to help the circulation in my numbing fingers, but I had a somehow superstitious feeling that if I did that, this clandestine meeting would never take place. We were already thirty minutes after the time specified in the note I'd received that morning at my office.

Before the mail came, I'd called Catherine at the apartment we share in the Kenwood area of Minneapolis that morning from my place in Roseville to tell her I was looking forward to fixing dinner later. It was another promise to my lady that was going unfulfilled. The list was growing. When the mail arrived it included a plain white metered envelope with no return address. Inside was a single piece of ordinary white typing paper folded around two more copied pages from a ledger. It took me only a moment to verify my instinct, these were identical to the copies I'd received a few days earlier.

On a separate half-sheet of paper was a printed note. It gave a time and a place, explicit instructions as to signals and doors, and suggested it would be useful for me to show up. Tracing the printer that placed the words on the paper or tracing the paper itself might be possible, but in the end probably not informative. When I suggested testing for fingerprints by the Minneapolis PD, I was met with overt skepticism that there would be anything to find. It was also suggested I turn everything I knew over to the FBI or the Secret Service and take a vacation down south.

I dialed Catherine at her massage school to cancel our dinner date. She was understanding. Of course I would show up for the meeting. The date was that night, the time was 1:30 in the morning and the place was an older, slightly seedy, office building on Chicago Avenue, on the south side of Minneapolis. My good friend, the aforementioned Detective Sergeant Ricardo Simon, agreed to accompany me as my armed backup. The note hadn't said to come alone.

So here we were now, half-frozen as the February temperature continued to fall, waiting for a light to flash in yonder window which was the signal I should cross the street and enter the door that faced me. I would be jaywalking in the middle of the block and there was no alley. Because of winter parking restrictions, there were no cars on either side of the street. I suppose somebody standing at one of the several dark windows in the five stories that faced me could be waiting with a rifle, but it just didn't feel like that kind of a setup. I tend to go with my gut feeling in these situations. Several friends have suggested that's foolish, but I'm still here, aren't I. Still scuffling around doing my job.

That's not to say I wasn't a little nervous. I would have preferred not to be there. After all, not too many miles away, in a warm and cozy place, my good friend Catherine Mckerney waited, holding in her warm hand a nice glass of single malt. And a warm welcoming smile reserved just for me.

Second floor, left corner. A light flashed twice in the curtainless window. After a brief pause, the signal came again. I stepped into the street, a dark blob shuffling across the snowy pavement. I was tense and tuned to the sound of an engine, in case that box truck tried for me again, but it would have to come around a corner from half a block away. Nothing happened except that I reached the designated door and went in. The steps only led down to the basement. It was dark and I went cautiously. Ricardo would stay in that doorway for five minutes and then follow me into who knew what?

"Hello?" No response.

Five steps down and I was in a long dim concrete corridor that seemed to split the block. I couldn't see the other end. There were some dim bulbs in ceiling sockets that didn't quite illuminate the space. Dim bulbs. I was another, slowly easing my way into the interior. I reached a door set flush in the concrete wall. The wall and the door and the painted door knob were all cold to my fingers. I stopped beside the door and reached out to slowly turn the knob. Except for my hand and forearm, I was protected by the wall.

I touched the knob and then I realized there was an identical wooden door directly across the corridor. Not good.

With eyes on the door across from me, and somewhat down the hall, I continued twisting the knob in hand, meeting no particular resistance until I tried to open the door. It was locked. I looked across the space at the other door. Two steps and I twisted an identical knob. This door too was locked. I continued down the long concrete corridor thinking this was ridiculous and I should leave. Soon I encountered another pair of doors opposite each other, both of which were locked. I judged I was now about halfway across the building. I couldn't quite see the end of the hallway. The whole situation was nerve-wracking.

Behind me came a harsh rattling noise that bounded off the concrete walls. It sounded just like someone trying to open a locked door. From the sound and the direction I figured it was Ricardo trying to enter the building from the same door I had used at the street level. A door that now was apparently locked.

Time to leave. My pulse was sky high and my heart was thumping a strong hot rhythm. I turned around and licked my suddenly dry lips. This was supposed to have been a meeting. To me that meant some other person would be present and we would exchange information, or lies, or maybe gunshots, but I was alone in the long hall. I decided to risk a quick trot to the far end of the hall.

Almost at the very end, in which appeared to be a metal door, I noticed a large thick envelope on the floor. The envelope was propped against the wall beside a third door. I leaned over the envelope and peered at it. The pounding behind me, from the door where I'd entered, sounded louder and more urgent.

I took my penlight from a side pocket and shined it on the package. I didn't see any wires. Then I turned my head away and with one foot, pushed the thing over so it fell on the floor. No flash, no noise, no explosion. I exhaled.

The sealed envelope had two large black S's on it. Printed in what looked like a black marker pen. I picked up the object and felt it. It was substantial enough to contain a quantity of something, paper, perhaps. The rattling noise came again, louder this time. I thought I heard a faint shout. I sprinted back down the corridor and ran up the stairs. Ricardo Simon, about to shoot a hole in the door frame, flinched as I appeared. When I pushed on the door, it opened easily. Of course.

"Damn, it! I was getting worried," he said.

"Me too. Part of me says I guess this is the way anonymous people want to play it. Another part says they've been reading too many bad spy novels."

"A possibility that occurs to me is this." Ricardo scratched his nose while he organized what he was going to say. I think he picked up the scratching habit from me. "Maybe whoever left the package wanted to see if and who might be your backup as well as provide some more information."

I blew out my breath and we turned the corner to where we'd parked my Taurus. "Do you feel like we need to check the car for a bomb?"

Ricardo looked at me and shrugged, reaching for the door handle. "In for a penny."

He yanked on the door which refused to budge.

"It's probably frozen shut. Does that sometimes."

I pulled strongly on the driver's side door and it swung open. Inside, I swiveled and slammed both feet against the inside of the other door. This time, when Ricardo pulled, it creaked open. It didn't get much use so I'd have to remember to spray the hinges every so often with WD-40.

I slid the key into the ignition and hesitated.

"Not enough time to rig something," Ricardo muttered.

I started the engine and nothing blew up.

Ricardo reached for the overhead light but there wasn't one. I removed it years ago. Helps keep me from getting potted by a sharpshooter at night. Or seen entering and exiting.

The dash compartment gave up my trusty Maglight and we put our heads together and examined the envelope. It was padded, white, about eleven by fourteen inches, dirty and smudged. There was some evidence that old labels had been removed. One end was sealed with beige masking tape. I slit the tape and eased the end open.

Ricardo was scanning the street when I said, "There are several sheets of paper in here, but I don't see any wires or powder or anything out of the ordinary."

"Okay. A white box truck just cruised by."

I jerked my head up to see the back end of such a vehicle disappearing down the block. "Let's make tracks."

"Or just haul ass," he cracked.

I dropped the envelope in his lap and we beat it out of there back to my office.

Chapter 18

My feet were just beginning to warm up with the car heater on full blast when we got to my office on Central. My watch read 2:45 as we shuffled down the dim hall. I stopped at the closed door and peered at the lock. I was tired, adrenalin bleeding out of me after my high-tension confrontation with the envelope in the basement of that office building. But I was also jazzed enough to want to see what was in the package.

He didn't say so, but I knew Ricardo well enough that I was sure he wanted a gander at the contents as well. Plus, being a cop he had to know whether I'd laid hands on vital evidence of some sort that might pertain to an active case of the homicide squad.

"What?" he said when I didn't open the door.

"My penlight's out of juice. You got one?"

Ricardo fished out a regulation-sized flash and aimed it at the door lock.

"Does that look okay to you?"

"Sean, you are getting paranoid." He bent for a closer look. "Yeah, it's fine. C'mon, open up."

I did. Inside I threw off my coat and gloves and said, "If I was a good, classic, P.I., I'd offer you some whiskey, or at least some coffee."

"Okay."

"Alas, I'm neither good nor classic. No booze and no coffee. Sorry."

Ricardo shrugged and I upended the envelope on my desk. What slid out were three white business sized envelopes and several folded pieces of paper. I reached into my desk drawer and found my tweezers and magnifying glass.

"I got gloves here," Ricardo grunted.

The drawer also contained a partly crushed box of tic tacs, which Ricardo waved away when I offered them.

The first envelope I tweezed open contained a stack of newspaper clippings. Copies. Somebody had dated most of them in pen or pencil but had not written the name of the newspaper, although as I picked through them, a few had dates from a Chicago paper and from the *Saint Paul Pioneer Press*. Another was a *Minneapolis Tribune* piece.

"Whoever collected these must be foreign born," Ricardo muttered.

"Why d'you say that?"

"Look at the way the dates are written. And the sevens."

"I wonder if these are originally from Manny Gottleib. Maybe his writing?" I said, then paused. "Look at this." I pushed over a letter from another envelope. The printing at the top indicated a war crimes organization of some sort, but the language was unfamiliar. "Polish, maybe? Russian?"

"Huh. It thanks the sender for the inquiry, but doesn't say what the subject is. It's dated July of 1953."

"That would be right after Gottlieb got to Minneapolis," I said. My eyes focused on another letter, but then things got a little blurred. I needed some serious sleep time. I shook my head and tweezed open another envelope. This one contained copies of articles from a newspaper neither of us could read. All were dated in script from mid 1954.

"What language is this?"

Ricardo lifted his hands. "No clue. Let me rephrase. I suspect the language is from eastern Europe somewhere. It could be Romanian." He pointed to a long name that seemed to have several m's and z's. "You'll need to get these translated. Prob'ly someone at the U could help."

I nodded and tweezed open the third envelope. The envelope contained a neat stack of pages I recognized. I spread them out. "I've seen these before," I muttered.

"Yes? How come?"

"They look like original pages from a ledger. I already have copies of pages from the same ledger."

"You're sure it's the same ledger?"

"Of course not," I said, "but, yes, I'm sure. Look." I pulled open my file drawer and fished out the copies Ann/Anne had sent to me.

Ricardo spent a couple of minutes bent over the copies and the pages, being careful to keep them in separate piles on my desk. He used my magnifying glass to peer at first one then another. Finally he looked up at me.

"Okay, I agree. These copies you say you got from your client Ann, are definitely from the same or an identical source. I'd say they're written in the same hand and even if we can't analyze the ink or the paper for comparison . . ."

"Agreed," I said. "Here's the deal." I filled him in on the client with the ledger and her apparent connection to the deceased Manfred Gottlieb.

"We'll require that the documents be turned over," Ricardo said. "Manny Gottlieb is an open case. If these papers can be linked to him, they belong in police custody."

"No problem. I'll just make copies for my files while you saunter down the hall to the men's room."

He did and I did and a few minutes later we had our heads together above the desk, staring down at the papers. "I haven't any more thoughts on this, have you?" I mumbled.

"Maybe we'll find some fingerprints we can use." He yawned. "It's almost dawn and I'm wiped. I have to drop these at the property room and make out an affidavit before I can head home." Ricardo gathered the material together and slid it back into the padded envelope. "Fortunately, I don't have a shift today."

We closed up my office and at the building entrance Ricardo and I touched gloved hands. "Thanks for backing me up," I said.

"Don't mention it," he responded with a tired smile. "But let me know if things develop."

He turned and went to his car. I followed him out of the lot and drove home to my house and cats. At least I think I did, because I woke up late the next morning in my Roseville bedroom with no real recollection of how I got there. Zoned out, or slept on the drive home. On automatic pilot. I hoped I hadn't killed anybody, or damaged somebody's property.

* * * *

NEAR NOON I left the house for the drive to Minneapolis. I did a thorough inspection of the Taurus. No ticket. No new bumps, dents or breaks. Apparently I'd managed to make it home in one piece. I hoped Ricardo had had similar good fortune.

At my office there was a single message on my answering machine. The elusive and mysterious Robert Gehrz, putative client, would materialize at one. He arrived at two minutes before the appointed hour. As at his previous and only visit, he was impeccably and expensively dressed for the season.

"Sit down, Mr. Gehrz."

"Thank you. I have limited time today, but it occurred to me you may be needing some additional funds to continue your search for Ms. Market. Unless you have found the woman I seek."

"Thank you. I do require some additional funds. There are certain inquiries I shall have to make that will involve the payment of funds. Besides which I have already spent a good deal of time on this effort. Let me lay it out for you."

I recapped in some detail what I had done to find the woman. "The address for the woman you seek is, as you must know, an upscale townhouse in Northeast Minneapolis. She has a lease that expires in June. The manager gave me a description of the woman that matches yours in every important aspect." Gehrz nodded.

The building manager admitted he hadn't seen the woman in quite a while, I explained, but there had been no complaints and all expenses associated with the space were current and always paid on time. In spite of a pecuniary inducement, I got no more from him. I told Gehrz that I left the building with the impression the guy would have said more if he'd known anything else. His gaze had followed the thick fold of Benjamins back into my pocket with what appeared to be considerable longing. Or maybe just avarice.

Gehrz said, "You paid the man a hundred dollars."

"I did. Probably one of those bills you paid me with initially."

"I see. Do go on."

I did, but I wondered fleetingly if Gehrz was concerned about the amount I'd paid, or that it might have been one of the same bills he'd paid me. I didn't ask.

"I was able to snare the names of some of the people living on the same floor. It seems they did not know Ms. Market very well. Really, not at all. None of them admitted to having seen or talked with her more than once or twice." I neglected to mention that none of them recognized the tall figure of a man in the other picture I showed them. The one I'd surreptitiously snapped of my client after he left my office the first time.

"There was one oddity."

Gehrz seemed to tense just slightly. "Really?"

"Yes, one of the tenants mentioned that he'd seen Ms. Market leaving the building in a long padded white coat with a thick hooded collar. In this climate, that's not so unusual, but since it was the second time he'd encountered her, he noted that this time she was also wearing a dark-brown wig."

"Whereas Tiffany is a blond," Gehrz acknowledged. "I assume you trust this information?"

"I do. They passed each other at the door to the elevator and he'd talked to her previously when she was without doubt the blond Ms. Market.

"I have also traced your Ms. Market to her former place of employment and, through various stratagems you needn't inquire about, I've determined that she's not been seen for some time in any of her usual places, including the health club where she was a regular. Near as I can place it, since you asked me to locate her last week."

"I see. And do you think you should continue my search?"

"That, of course, is ultimately up to you, but if I do I will find the woman or if it happens that she's left the Twin Cities, I'll determine that as well."

"I see. Since I am more anxious than ever to find her, let's continue." Gehrz's lips under his sandy mustache twitched and he reached into an inside pocket. Out came a brown envelope. I was betting it was the same one he'd been carrying the other time we met. He fished out more Benjamins and laid another two grand on the desk top. Once again, with the tips of his fingers, he slid them toward me. He had a peculiar way of handling the bills and I was willing to bet there weren't any useful fingerprints to be found on any of the money, should I look. I read somewhere that agents employed in covert roles in foreign countries were taught how to handle money smoothly without leaving fingerprints.

"Is there anything else on your mind, Mr. Sean?"

I shrugged. I had a lot on my mind but nothing I wanted to share. Gehrz stood up and slung his coat over his shoulder on the way out. He didn't say goodbye.

Chapter 19

"Are you ready to go?"

"Shoes," I said. "Or boots?"

"I'm going to wear my snow boots and carry shoes. We'll park under cover at both ends, so no slogging through slush, but—"

"You're afraid I might get us stuck on these city streets," I said.

Catherine smirked at me. "Just being prepared."

I went to the front entrance and smiled up at my lady. Catherine was examining herself critically in the full-length mirror, heels and all. The smart heels put her at just over six-three. You'd expect a massage expert to avoid heels, but sometimes fashion rules all. She had chosen to wear a silk satiny deep-maroon blouse over a long black skirt that swung just above the floor. The blue shawl added a nice accent.

The rubber heels on my black soft-soled slip-ons put me at just over five-two. The tassels didn't count. I was wearing my standard single-breasted black suit over a figured white dress shirt, complete with black onyx studs in gold settings. We made an outstanding looking couple on the social scene.

The holster for my piece was strapped snugly to my left ankle. The holster, made of soft supple kidskin with nice comfortable straps, was an expensive affair. I'd figured Catherine had come to terms with my hardware when the holster showed up as a Christmas gift. But she still didn't let me store a heavier gat in her new Lexus. She didn't like the odor, she said.

I slipped out of my dress shoes and into my galoshes. Catherine grinned and held my overcoat for me. Unless there was a chair or stool close by, it was nearly always impossible for me to do the gentlemanly thing and hold her coat. We'd come to terms with that a long time ago.

Out the door, along the hall, we turned right to the elevator shaft, and down into the garage. I didn't think it showed, but my nerves twanged when Catherine didn't hesitate, just shot out the door into the garage.

I had the key in hand and we made our way smoothly out of the space and into a snowy evening. So, what else is new?

The gala we were headed to was a civic affair of some kind in the ballroom at the Hilton Hotel in downtown Minneapolis. We were gathering to drink and smooze and congratulate ourselves for meeting some fund-raising goal.

I'd debated ordering a cab or a limo but I have a tendency to want a little more control than that. After all, a lot of my moxie, my presence, and my success, comes from being the little man who wasn't there. Even in circumstances where I've been employed for temporary security, I've almost always been the least noticeable, and that's not just because I'm a shrimp in the height and weight department. I discovered early on that people of "normal" height tend to overlook those who are shorter, unless they make a fuss. Being the little dude who wasn't there has been useful and even instructive at times.

The congratulatory gathering was in one of the Hilton's smaller ballrooms. The hotel had laid on a couple of cash bars stocked with comely bartenders and an upscale selection of wines and stronger potables. We weren't the first to arrive and the tip jars were already well-stuffed. As is the usual custom at these shindigs, couples arrived, made a quick survey, usually grabbed a drink and then split to personal interactions. Social networks being what they were, the couple frequently connects with people one of the partners may not even know. Catherine had a wide circle of acquaintances and associates. I had few. Moreover, the ones I did know quite often didn't want it known they knew me, or I them. That left me free to offer occasional subtle nods across the room, and to circulate alone with a drink in my hand and listen to the conversations. In a word, eavesdrop. Information, after all, is the primary currency of the detective biz.

Thus it was I clearly heard a portly man of florid complexion and a too-loud voice standing off to my left, intone to his companion, a fellow of saturnine hue, "I think we oughta bomb them. Blast 'em back to the Stone Age. Too many of our so-called leaders are way too willing to compromise."

"Did you hear about the looting?"

"You mean in Baghdad, at the museums?"

"Right. You'd think after what happened in Europe during World War Two, the military would have learned a lesson."

The portly man gulped his drink and shook his head. "I'm on the board of the art museum, the big one here in Minneapolis, you know. We've been dealing with that recently."

"Stolen art?"

"Somebody donated a painting back in the early sixties, I guess. Got a nice tax write off for it, of course. Now some kid is claiming it was stolen from his family by the Nazis. He wants it returned."

"Can he prove ownership?"

"Huh," snorted portly florid, "not likely. Those people were the hoi polloi when war broke out and some of them supported Hitler at first. Least, that's what I hear. If their goods got confiscated, maybe they just got what they deserve. So where do they get off claiming ownership now? If we have to return the painting it's gonna cost the museum a bundle."

I pivoted slowly away as the men moved off. I didn't recognize the voices and I hadn't recognized either when I first saw them. It was pretty clear to me who the 'they' and 'those people' the jerk was referring to. I didn't think Catherine or the organizers of this event would appreciate my decking the guy in the middle of the room. Instead, I went to the bar across the room and got a drink of scotch, one ice cube, no water.

A little while later I watched while Catherine was briefly recognized for a noticeable donation to the cause. When she mounted the low platform to receive a polite round of applause, her gaze sought mine and I saluted her with my glass. I noted that the chairwoman of the event managed to credit Catherine for her donation without revealing exactly how she acquired enough money to make such a generous gift and maintain the good life.

The evening passed without incident and we drove home through the deeply frigid night air. When we arrived in the garage below the apartment building, I made Catherine wait in the car while I did a quick survey of the space. We then took the elevator to our apartment and to our bed. Life did not intrude and we were undisturbed until the bedside alarm sounded in the gray light of early dawn.

Chapter 20

I'D HAD A TELEPHONE LINE installed in the apartment that was essentially an extension of my office phone. I had another in my house in Roseville. That way I could do some business if needed without being in my office. Yes, I know about cell phones. I've even considering buying one, but like my gats and my filing system, some things just require a certain comfort level. Leaping along with the latest technology doesn't always fulfill one's basic needs. Someday I might even succumb and purchase a laptop computer.

I was on my third cup of coffee, scanning the morning newspaper when the phone rang. My office line has a distinctive ring. I picked up.

"Good morning. Sean Sean, private investigations. How may I serve?"

"This is Aaron." The voice was gravelly, as if the caller had just awoken from a long sleep with his mouth open the whole time.

"Aaron?"

"Yeah, Aaron. Jeeze. How many Aaron's you know? Gottlieb. Aaron Gottlieb. Manny's grand nephew?"

Testy testy. "Sure, Mr. Gottlieb. How are you today?"

"Rotten. I'd just been talking to your police department up there."

"I see."

"They aren't being helpful. They don't appear to be making any progress. And they aren't telling me anything."

"I'm sure they'd tell you if there was anything to report." I was pretty sure the cops wouldn't tell him zip until they were ready. "This is a difficult case and I'm sure they're doing everything they can."

"It's been a couple of days and nobody's even called. You haven't called, either."

"Exactly. It's been a very short while and there are lots of details to look into. Leads to follow."

"You have some leads to the killer?" He sounded eager.

"It takes time to build a case, to find enough evidence to nail a killer."

"Yeah, but—"

How did I get to be a police apologist all of a sudden? "Look, Aaron, you have to be patient about this. And while I have you on the phone, I do have a couple of questions." Pause. Silence. "Aaron?"

"What?"

"Have you noticed anything unusual since your—since Mr. Gottlieb was killed?"

"Like what?"

"I don't have anything specific. I just wondered. Somebody who seems to be watching or following you. Unexplained changes in the routines of people around you, like the mailman?" I didn't want to put ideas in his head, but since Catherine and I were both feeling watched sometimes, I thought I'd ask him. Since he'd called me anyway.

"You think somebody's following me?"

"Didn't say that, did I?"

He sounded a little sharper now. "My land line went out sometime yesterday. And after the repair guy came, the sound is fuzzy. You're fuzzy."

"Are they coming back to repair it?"

"Yeah, any time now. Do you think somebody bugged my phone? Why would they do that?"

"No, Aaron, I don't think anybody bugged your phone. I can hear you just fine." Unfortunately. "Listen, you just hang in there and relax. I promise I'll call you just as soon as anything concrete develops."

"Yeah, well, I guess." Gottlieb hung up without saying goodbye. He'd sounded a little depressed. It was possible the people who killed his great-uncle were watching Aaron as well. But my sense, based on almost nothing, was that the focus was here in the Twin Cities.

The next time the telephone sounded I didn't recognize the voice of the woman. Then she said her name was Ursula. Ursula Skranslund.

"I apologize," I said when she identified herself. "I know you had to find someplace to stay after the fire and I should have followed up with you."

"No problem, Mr. Sean. I've been staying with friends. They had an extra bedroom after somebody moved out. We're all grad students. It's a little more friendly now that I'm not rattling around in a big house all alone. I guess a house of grad students is a little quieter than a dorm or a house of undergraduates. This one is, anyway."

"Can I buy you a cup of coffee, or a dessert, maybe?"

No hesitation. "Gee, that would be nice. You mean today? What time?"

I hadn't exactly figured my offer would be so promptly accepted, but my schedule wasn't jammed this day so we arranged to meet at a small diner on Lake Street near the river. It was only a couple of blocks from her address, she said.

Half an hour later we sat at a small table in one corner of the place which wasn't much bigger than a minute. I've heard that phrase applied to people, pets and places, but I'm not sure where it came from or what it really means. Size aside, the diner had a neighborhood reputation as a top pie place. In fact, that's what it was called—The Pie Place. I had a big slice of banana cream pie with about two inches of whipped cream on top, the kind my momma used to make from thick cream, sugar, and vanilla, whipped thick with an eggbeater. Ursula was eating apple pie with a dollop of ice cream and a slab of cheese.

"Thanks for this," she said between bites.

"You obviously enjoy eating apple pie, and I'm pleased things are going well for you. I did wonder if you've had any thoughts about your former housemate."

"Not really. Mr. Gottlieb was always nice and even formal, like I told you before. Or I guess you'd say polite."

"I'm afraid we, and I include the police here, haven't made much progress finding his murderer."

"I'm sorry. It's sad that after so much tragedy in his life in Poland, he couldn't find a little peace during his last years. Which reminds me, I meant to tell you earlier that I've had two people asking about him."

"Police?"

She shook her head. "I don't think so. Once a man came to the house. He said he was an insurance adjuster. He wanted to know where the contents of the house had been taken after the fire."

"I wasn't aware they'd moved things out."

"Yeah. The building inspector came and I met him at the house. He said they'd have to condemn it. I didn't think it was that bad, but the whole place smelled pretty awful."

"Did this inspector show you some credentials?"

There was a pause while Ursula swallowed another forkful of apple pie. She looked at me with those wise Finnish eyes and then said. "Oh, yes. That's part of what I meant to tell you. The city guy showed me his identification right away. But the other guy—"

"The one who said he was an insurance investigator?"

"Yes, I had to fuss a little. Then he showed me a business card. It seemed legit, but anybody can print a business card, right?

I nodded. Little did Ursula know that at that very moment, my card case in one pocket contained at least four cards in four different names, and four different professions, all with a thumbnail picture of yours truly.

"You're right, of course," I sighed. "There are people everywhere carrying false identification."

"Well, in the end it didn't matter all that much. Aaron Gottlieb had left me a message telling where the contents of the house were stored and what I had to do to get my stuff released."

I raised an interrogatory eyebrow. It's something I practice.

"All the contents of the house that's left is in a security warehouse over in Northeast. When I went to get my belongings, I had to sign some papers and prove who I was. I got the impression it would be pretty hard for someone to get into the place without a legitimate reason."

I was reassured that if there was anything still in Gottlieb's possession when he died, Aaron and I had missed it and it was still amongst the belongings, or it had flown away before I got there. Did that mean I should go look again? I was of two minds. Since I still wasn't one-hundred per cent sure what I was looking for, it might be a monumental waste of time. But the appearance of a phony insurance adjuster—yes, I was morally certain the guy who'd approached Ursula was not legit—told me that some somebodies were still out there searching.

I thanked Ursula for the company and the info. She thanked me for the pie and the conversation. I went home to Kenwood to ponder my next move.

Chapter 21

I woke up feeling mildly discouraged. In my mind I replayed my chat with Aaron Gottlieb. I decided I was the one who'd sounded paranoid. I may have agitated the poor guy even more than he was before he called me. Just the thing a good P.I. should be doing. Then I replayed the conversation I'd overheard the previous evening at the fund-raising gala for that foundation. The conversation from the overweight florid-looking fellow who was on the MIA board. It was entirely too convenient that his conversation dealt with an area of life I was presently rooting around in. I say rooting because so far things were still very directionless. By this time I was usually trotting along a very specific trail that would eventually lead to a specific conclusion. Not always the last or even the best solution, you understand, but often that was the case.

So, of all the people at that affair I might have been overhearing, why was it that bozo? My gut told me there was a reason. I usually listened to my gut, particularly when, as now, it was sending signals that I should take in some protein. I went to the kitchen, fried me an egg and some low-fat, relatively tasteless, sausages and a piece of toast. Then I called Catherine.

"Hey, babe."

"Think about the other night at the ball," I said. A preparatory ploy.

"Okay." She was used to my verbal ploys.

"There was a man there whose name I now need."

"Seriously? Wow, there's probably a guest list available, but . . ." Her voice trailed off.

"I can describe the man. He is large, was formally dressed in a good quality dark suit. Florid. He'll probably die of a heart problem before many more years pass. His well-shorn hair, all his own I judged, was going to gray. He's on the board of MIA and I got the impression his political views are conservative. Probably in his sixth decade."

"Hmm, doesn't ring any bells. Let me make a few calls for you," she said.

"Thanks." We hung up and I had another cup of coffee and read the morning paper. I also stared out the kitchen window at the overcast day. The news wasn't good and nothing seemed likely to bolster my spirits. Maybe a good massage from one of Catherine's students would help.

The telephone beeped. It was my office line again, so I picked up.

"Murchison. Albert Murchison is his name," Catherine said.

"No shit!" I exclaimed. "What a fantastic coincidence."

"Life does that at times. I take it you're pleased with the information."

"You bet."

"There is more. He recently went on the institute's board. His family is wealthy. They are powerful politically and in other ways in Minnesota and have been here a very long time. Mr. Murchison is in manufacturing and his younger brother is a lawyer in a firm you know. This Albert Murchison sits on a lot of corporate boards."

"Harcourt, Saint Martin, Saint Martin, Bryce, et cetera," is the law firm, I said.

"Correct."

"Anything else?"

"Gossip, rumors, as there always is about important people in the community."

"Sure. Tell."

"A long time ago a Murchison donated an important piece of art, an oil painting, to the museum. It was worth a great deal of money at that time. More now, I assume."

"In the millions?"

"Easily."

My gut was bouncing in restrained and premature glee. "And?"

"Well, now a question of provenance has come up. I'm repeating gossip, you understand. You know what provenance is, I assume. Path of ownership, that sort of thing."

"I get it. If there are questions relating to legitimacy of ownership, clouds gather. I bet there are actions being quietly taken to figure out how to make the questions go away."

"I suppose so," Catherine said. "What does this have to do with you?"

"Suppose the donor of the object in question, the painting, was able to arrange for the painting to be quietly returned up the line to someone whose ownership was unquestioned? Wouldn't that be easier to do that if the returner was an institution, rather than an individual? Would that make the questions go away?"

I heard silence on the line while Catherine pondered.

You might not think it, but Catherine Mckerney, expert massage therapist and business woman, has more entrée to the convoluted world of wealthy folks and social manipulators than do I. In the past I have used her insight and connections to advantage.

"Yes, I suppose it would," she said. "The institution could simply insist the donor's identity had to be protected for the deal to go through."

"It would be a little trickier if the original donation to the institution was publically acknowledged. But it would work if somebody close to the original donor was in a position of power and had, wink wink, plausible deniability."

"I'm sure you're right. I have to go. Hope I've helped, my morose friend."

She clicked off and I was left to ponder that last remark. Apparently I had not been as successful at dissembling my feelings the last few days. I'd have to practice on that. Meantime, there was new information to consider.

The Murchison name had appeared earlier. In one of my conversations with attorney Madison, he had mentioned the name of that very family. Was there an older link between the name Murchison and art and between Gottlieb and Murchison or . . .

The possibilities were extensive, not to say endless. Research was called for. With a rising sense of excitement I toddled off to my office and my ancient computer. I would be delving with the Dell for several hours.

There were no recorded messages, there were no phone calls and no visitors so I was able to concentrate for a couple of hours. I went to various sites for which I paid some serious money to winkle out tidbits of information. For example, a Murchison family of no remarkable attributes had shown up on a city census as early as 1890. The patriarch of the family listed his occupation as laborer.

I followed the family, living in Minneapolis, through a number of generations. I was able to discover that several Murchisons from the family I was researching had been in the military service. One of them had been assigned to an unspecified unit somewhere in Poland. Probably a liaison of some kind to the Russians. That assignment was short because less than a year later, in 1946, Arthur Murchison was mustered out and came home to Minneapolis and, presumably, to the relieved and welcoming bosom of his wife and two small sons.

Four years later, Arthur Murchison was considerably wealthier. I was able to deduce this from the fact that he moved from a nice but ordinary home on the north side of Minneapolis to the hamlet of Wayzata. Anyone who has even a little familiarity with the Twin Cities knows Wayzata is mostly made up of important and pretty well-off movers and shakers.

Further, Mr. Murchison was now the manager or CEO of a small but active machine parts manufacturer, as well as one of the owners. In the space of a very few years, Mr. Murchison had become a minor if significant player. His sons had apparently inherited the family penchant for successfully making money out of other money. A few years later, the Murchison family owned the manufacturing plant outright. More power to them, I figured. My curiosity and interest focused on that initial jump from North Minneapolis to owner-slash-CEO of a manufacturing company.

I decided I needed a higher level of expertise in the history and activities of corporate America. I needed a hacker. I ambled down the hall to the office of my friends and occasional associates, Belinda and Betsey Revulon. These two large and lush ladies of Scandinavian extraction were computer competents of the highest order. Their business, designing and operating large databases and programs for corporate clients, was beyond my comprehension, but I had yet to find a data storage problem they could not penetrate. I occasionally wondered if they sometimes hacked into our government systems just for the fun of it. I never asked.

The cousins had adopted me as a sort of pet. They felt they looked after me as one should, of a short-statured fellow. When the luscious blond Belinda threw her arms around me, I was often crushed into the considerable valley of her bosom in a way that made my lungs protest.

Chapter 22

Belinda, her feet up on the desk, and her ample lap cradling a wireless keyboard, smiled a happy greeting. "Welcome! I see by the look on your face you'd like some help."

I explained my need, all the while trying to avoid staring at her exposed cleavage. "One more thing," I said. "Be especially reticent about this one." Reticent was a code word we occasionally used to signify something particularly sensitive.

After Belinda received my background information she nodded and said, "Okay. What you want to know is where did this Art Murchison get the moolah to go into manufacturing. And the period is between 1946 and 1950. Correct?"

"Yes, thank you."

"Hokay! I'll get back to you soon as I have anything worth the while."

Dismissed, I went back to my office down the empty hall, pausing only once. Hokay? Where had that come from?

When I pondered something, that is think hard about something significant, I tended to look at the floor or the ground. Especially so when I'm walking. Somewhere safe. Thus it was when I came to my office door I saw on the tile a small speck of mud and water. It couldn't have been there long because the hallway was warm enough to melt snow, even if the manager of the place liked to use small light bulbs in the overhead fixtures to conserve energy. The floors were swept nightly and swabbed and polished as needed. Frequently in winter.

I bent lower and scanned the floor. A little way along I found another speck of watery mud. This one was larger and there was even a trace of icy snow. In a shot I leapt to the window just beyond the elevator door and scanned what I could see of the parking lot behind our building. Cars but no foot traffic appeared. I went back to my office and stood to one side as I twisted the doorknob and pulled the door open. No sound emanated from my digs.

I exhaled and went inside and closed the door. Standing just inside, I stared carefully at the entire room. Nothing appeared disturbed. I paid particular attention to my desk top. I did not routinely leave my office unlocked, nor did I leave important papers lying out. So what was I alarmed about?

Since the beginning of this dance with the death of Gottlieb and the missing Market woman, this affair had been swaddled in an odd atmosphere. I went to my desk and eased into my chair, all the while looking closely at the drawer pulls. I couldn't remember the last time a fed had paid me a visit. I bet if I really looked, I wouldn't find a single incident, beyond the one the other day. Likewise, I could count on two fingers the times I'd had any meaningful interaction with attorney at law, Mr. Derrol Madison, esquire. They had both come during my inquiries into the Gottlieb affair and my tenuous client, Anne/Ann of unknown last name, mysterious conductor of random pieces of ledger paper.

I extracted my pile of note cards from my desk and shuffled through them, adding a bit here and there. I jotted down information regarding the Murchison clan and the art world. Then I sat back and waited. For inspiration, for a phone call, for a white box truck to show up in the alley. None of that happened for quite some time. I expect I dozed off once or twice.

I debated whether I should call one of the lawyers I knew at Harcourt, St. Martin, Bryce, et cetera to probe for Murchison family gossip. I decided I needed more background before that would be helpful.

At 3:00 p.m. the telephone rang and my cases began to come together.

"I have something for you, sweetums." Belinda Revulon's voice carried smug overtones.

"I'm on my way."

"Once again, you will not be asking for sources, will you." Belinda's voice was now flat and serious, sounding as she regarded me over the top edge of her monitor screen. It was not a question.

"I'm okay with that."

"We're very clean and reticent here." Reticent was a code word I'd adopted when I wanted the Revulons to be especially careful to avoid leaving any traces of their electronic probing. When one of them said things were clean, I knew they'd gone and done whatever it was they went and did whatever it was they did, and no one would find a trace leading back to them. I had no idea how that all worked and had zero curiosity about it.

"Your subject borrowed money against an art object. Probably a painting. The piece apparently hung on a bank officer's wall for a while but has long since been retrieved."

"A lot of money?"

Shrug, which set a lot of bare flesh to quivering. "Depends on your meaning. On today's market, the amount is not large. In 1949 it was significant. Enough to buy a controlling interest in a very nice medium-sized manufacturing operation."

"Ah," I nodded. "A manufacturing operation that now carries a sign proclaiming Murchison Manufacturing. Any description of the painting?"

"Nothing meaningful. Even the painter's name appears to be redacted in the documents."

"And no provenance."

"Gee, Sean, you know some big words."

I smiled, thanked my benefactor, and toddled back to my office. So art. How much was anybody willing to bet the art in question was the same piece that old Al Murchison had used to back that loan of so long ago? The big question lodging itself in my brain was where had old Art Murchison laid hands on that piece of art? There were associated questions. Like, from whom and when.

Naturally, it could all be perfectly legal and on the up and up. Probably was. Well, I'd make some inquiries, because if the painting came through the hands of Art's granddaddy, a man not known for his strict adherence to the straight and narrow, it might be the same one that Arthur was referring to in the conversation I had overheard. I made another note card and reached for my coat and hat. It was getting late and in February in the Northland darkness came early.

I called Detective Ricardo Simon to advise him I had received another payment, this time with no additional pages copied from the elusive ledger. I gave him a couple of opportunities to update me on his analysis of the papers in the package from the basement, but he adroitly deflected the question by explaining that they still had no active leads on the murder of Manny Gottlieb and unless something broke pretty soon, the case would lose some of its priority status.

I'd learned through my many years in the detective business that late afternoons often found targets at a lower ebb, energy-wise. When one has had a full day at the office, one's ability to maintain an acceptable level of alertness and deal with impertinent probes from nosy private investigators was sometimes not high enough. That can apply to private investigators as well and that may be why I skipped naked out of the office. That is to say, I was unarmed.

Chapter 23

My office on Central Avenue, physically on the edge of the city's near north side, was only eight snowy blocks from Murchison Manufacturing. I slid into the single open visitor's parking slot in the well-plowed lot beside the beige painted cinderblock building. Small signs directed me to the proper entrance and into the lobby I went. In the back of my mind I registered that tiny snowflakes were beginning to sift down from gray skies.

The receptionist was a nicely set up female person of indeterminate age. She smiled and asked me how she could be of help.

"I'd like a few minutes with the owner, Mr. Murchison?"

"Have you an appointment?"

"No, I'm afraid not but I won't take up more than a very few minutes of his time."

Frown appeared on her smooth brow. "I'm afraid you must have an appointment to see Mr. Murchison."

I opened my mouth to protest but she went on without pause. "However, I see Mr. Murchison's second in command is still in the building. Perhaps he can help?"

"Sure. I'll start there. Could I have his name?"

"Yes, it's—oh, Mr. Murchison."

She was looking past me. A man had come into the lobby from somewhere in the building. He stood half way into the lobby with the door open. I could hear the sounds of machinery emanating from behind him. Second in command? Yet another Murchison?

"This gentleman wanted to see Mr. Murchison, senior. But he has no appointment. Perhaps you have a minute to help him?"

She smiled, rather sweetly, I thought, but there was something else in her tone. I looked across the lobby. This was definitely not the man I had observed at the recent arts fundraiser, but I noticed family traits. This Murchison was younger, weighed less and had reddish blonde hair. A son perhaps?

"Sure, I have a few minutes. Let's go to my office, Mr.—"

He put out his hand and since I had by now strode the few steps across the small lobby, we shook. His handshake was firm but not crushing and his hand was dry and smooth.

"Sean Sean," I said quietly, watching his eyes. There was just the tiniest flicker there. It could have been because of my names, but it could have been something else.

He led me through the door, which closed behind us with a quiet snick and we walked a few steps to an office. It was an ordinary square-shaped office with narrow windows high up at the eaves. Burglar proof, I judged, unless you were an unusually small person.

"Now, Mr. Sean, is it? You'll have to excuse me. I don't believe I've ever met anyone before with the same first and last names." He smiled and waved me to a seat beside his massive gleaming wooden desk.

"That's quite all right. I'm used to it. And to the reactions."

"Well, how can I help you?"

I fished out a business card that identified me as Sean Sean, Independent Scholar-slash-historian. It was a fresh card and when I handed it over, I had a momentary niggle that the ink might smear.

"I'm making inquiries of a historical nature about World War Two. I'm focusing on some local veterans who were involved in actions outside of the major, celebrated, battles. I've been led to believe your father was a soldier in Europe?" An old detective trick. I think I learned it reading Richard Prather. Or it might have been from something by Michael Connolly. The trick is to make some inconsequential mistake because it lowers your target's suspicion or their wall of resistance, when your target is the individual being questioned. I knew very well it couldn't be this bozo's father, it was his grandfather who served in the army in Europe during the Second World War.

Murchison—I didn't yet have his first name—grinned and shook his head. I could almost see him relaxing. Parenthetically the question was, what did this guy have to be tense about in the first place? He hadn't reacted to my name in any abnormal way He shouldn't be tense at all, unless he already knew why I was there. Anyway, he grinned and said, "No, Mr. Sean. I'm afraid it wasn't my father, that would be my granddad. Albert Murchison."

I nodded and made a note.

"Was your fath—sorry—grandfather named Albert Henry Murchison?"

"Umm, I think so. I just always called him Granddad, you know?"

"Sure, and your father, also named Albert, correct? So I guess that makes you Al Junior, yes?" I grinned disarmingly, I hoped.

"That would be my uncle. He's Albert, son of my grandfather and brother to my father, of course. My name, however, is Clem Albert Murchison. It does get confusing for some folks, I guess. The name goes back on my father's side for many generations."

Clem. "Would that be short for Clemenceau? I just want to be correct here. I hope I'm not prying." Was I being too obsequious?

"That's correct. I'm surprised. Few people make the connection. My mother's family is French and I guess there's a family connection."

"Well, your grandfather was in the army during World War Two and he was in the signal corps, and if my information is correct, he spent most of his active duty in the European Theater." I paused for a reaction. Murchison just looked at me. He didn't nod, or frown or anything. So I barreled on.

"Can you recall what unit he was attached to? Was it the U.S. Eighth Army Group?"

Again, a small error. It could take some digging but most servicemen's duty assignments, right down to the squad, if they were infantry, can be traced. The name of the unit I gave was wrong. It wasn't in Europe until after the surrender of all German forces. I hoped Murchison would correct me and save me the trouble of a long search. It would have been better talking to the old man, this one's grandfather, but sometimes you take what you can get.

"These are details I'm not really up on, Mr. Sean, but I think he was part of a signal corps unit that landed in Europe well after D-Day and he worked in Northern France and, I think, Belgium. For quite a while. Always in liberated territory, you see, after the Germans had been pushed out."

"Some time in 1944 he was transferred with a small unit to Poland, is that not correct?"

Murchison frowned as if my question might have made him a wee bit uncomfortable. It should, if he knew his granddad's entire history in the late stages of the war in that theater.

"Yes, that's correct. But he was only there a short while before Berlin fell and the war was over. Then Russian units replaced his and he came home. He was discharged soon after."

"Was he stationed near Lodz, do you remember?"

Deeper frown. "I really can't recall. But I don't think—oh, wait, in fact, Granddad was stationed for a few weeks in a small town outside of Warsaw. Northwest of the city, I think. I'm afraid I can't tell you the exact name."

Right. We sparred about a few more bits of information and I never asked him about how his grandfather had suddenly come up with the money to buy a share in the manufacturing operations I could faintly hear going on behind the walls that surrounded us.

Finally, about the time I was running out of seriously useful questions, Murchison glanced at his watch and said, "I'm afraid I have some pressing business, Mr. Sean, so we'll have to end this meeting. However, if you have additional questions, be sure to contact us again. In fact, I'll pass along your card to my father. He might have more useful knowledge for you than I do." He smiled, we stood and shook hands and I left.

I left wondering why Murchison was as conversant as he was about his grandfather's service in the world war. I was pretty sure most grandkids had only vague knowledge of their elder's military service. Was Murchison a world war buff? Or was there another reason?

Chapter 24

My interview with Clem Murchison was not one of the most productive I have ever conducted. That wasn't because Mr. Murchison was not forthcoming or because he was good at deflecting my probes. It was because once again in this case I felt the earth moving beneath me. Metaphorically, of course. I didn't know why but I sensed I needed more background information that I could piece out as needed, in order to rattle the cages of some of these people. If my clients had been more forthcoming in the beginning, we might have made faster progress and things might have turned out differently. As it was, I just wasn't ready to expose some of them to possible harm by talking about them. I needed a serious face to face with both Gehrz and Market and probably with Aaron Gottlieb as well. I was almost ready to put down a serious bet on the proposition that all of these people were somehow connected.

I stepped out of the entrance to Murchison Manufacturing into the darkness of a late February day. It had gotten colder and my breath bloomed in front of my face. Snow fell more thickly. The parking lot now held only a few scattered cars, including mine. The Taurus started okay and I pulled slowly into a mostly deserted street. The buildings along the street, all commercial and small business places, were internally dark, except for an occasional night light. I didn't notice anybody on the street.

The intersection sported a four-way stop sign. After I followed the rule, I accelerated peacefully into the space. I figure I was two thirds of the way across when headlights exploded in my left side window, highlighting snow in the air. The vehicle was maybe thirty feet away and already coming fast. My reflexes took over.

My foot bottomed out on the accelerator and the engine wound up. I'm sure the wheels spun on the pavement. There was a crash behind me and the rear left window disintegrated in just the way it would if struck by a large caliber bullet. I never heard the shot. An instant later the onrushing vehicle skidded into the rear fender of my car. The impact sent me and the Taurus rocketing on two wheels into a large snow bank up almost on its side. Had the snow bank not been there, the car would have gone over on its side or top. My head snapped back at the impact, and now I fell forward and instinctively jammed myself low toward the empty passenger's seat. The lunge took me below the top edge of the seatbacks and put my left hand within easy reach of the .32 caliber Chief's Lightweight Special I kept in a quick release holder under the dashboard. It's not the weapon I favor. A short barrel makes accurate shooting problematical. I released the seatbelt and grabbed the gat, sliding down toward the right-hand door. The revolver was loaded. It was always loaded with six slugs.

My passenger-side door didn't work well and it took me a few seconds to lever it open, pushing against the piled snow. When I wedged it open far enough to slide out, I took a swift gander back over my shoulder. The vehicle that had slammed into me had careened into another snow bank across the street. It appeared the driver had intended to drive up beside me and gun me down, then disappear, but slippery streets and maybe a nervous trigger finger had changed the scenario. Despite its size the driver had lost control of his truck for just long enough, shooting at me and then smashing into my poor car. Now he was snow-bound, gunning the engine, trying to get unstuck. Smoke billowed from the spinning tires of the white unmarked box truck and it shuddered and bucked but seemed to be well-stuck.

I half fell farther out of my car into the dirty snow and crouched by the rear wheel. The truck's driver-side window was half way down and suddenly a flash of light bloomed just above the top edge of the window. I instantly recognized a muzzle-flash. The bozo was shooting at me. Again.

I returned fire. Twice. Bullets cost money and I didn't have an unlimited supply in my ride so indiscriminate shooting was not on the agenda. In addition, bullets flying about a populated neighborhood could do serious if unintended damage to innocent bystanders. I hoped anybody in the nearby buildings behind me was ducking for cover. So was I. The truck engine revved to a brief scream and then coughed and died. I rose to one knee and bolted across the pavement, almost slipping on my ass on frozen snow in the middle of the intersection.

I slid to a stop by the side of the truck. The Taurus was still idling away there in its own snow bank behind me but all I heard from the box truck was the ticking sounds characteristic of a hot engine cooling down. In the distance and drawing closer, police sirens came to my ears. Putting a gloved hand on the side of the truck, I scuttled cautiously closer to the door. I panted, my breath loud in my ears. When the door handle was in reach I half-squatted and yanked with my left hand. Right hand steadied the revolver trained on the dark entrance to the cab. Not graceful and not orthodox but it got the job done.

Nothing happened except the door swung open, helped by the fact that the right side front wheel was up off the pavement in the snow. I peered around the door jam and saw the guy. He was slumped back with his chin on his chest. In his lap rested one hand with a big semi-auto—it looked like a Ruger .45. The sirens were closer now, a mere block or two away. Somebody'd been Johnny-on-the-spot with a 911 call. Not much time for a search.

The driver was dead. Damn it. I might have learned something significant, like why had he tried twice to run me over? And who was paying him? I ran my hand over his coat and pants pocket, trying for a wallet or any sort of ID. Nothing. I forced my concentration on the job at hand. I'd just killed a man, not something I did very often and I didn't like it at all.

A patrol car skidded into the intersection as I stepped back and dropped my revolver onto the pavement beside me. Then I turned around and faced the young officer who sprang out of her ride and came toward me, one hand on her holster.

"Stand still," she barked.

I wasn't moving, just stood there, both hands palms out at shoulder height. I tried hard to control the tremors running down my arms. Other patrol cars arrived in a flurry of engine noise, sirens and flashing lights.

"My weapon is on the ground at my feet," I told the officer. "I shot the driver of the truck. He was armed and he shot at me first. His weapon is in his lap. I'm pretty sure he's dead." I stared into her eyes and it appeared she understood what I was saying, that the danger was over and weapons weren't a threat anymore. These situations are always fraught because adrenalin is running and itchy fingers sometimes twitch.

I shifted my gaze from the closest officer to a big cop leaning on the other side of his vehicle staring at me. That was all right, but he was idly stroking his shotgun. The barrel was pointing at the sky, but if he threw down on us in a panic, he'd take both me and the officer out of this life in an instant.

The cop slipped her cuffs off her belt and her eyes sought the weapon at my feet. "Who are you?"

"Name's Sean Sean. I'm licensed to carry." My legs were starting to tremble. "I need to sit down before I fall over," I said.

She nodded and hollered for help. Now units swarmed around the intersection and then a big black Ford showed up with a pair of detectives I didn't recognize. After that, things got calm and quickly organized. Several cops set about securing the scene, doing the routine procedures required at a shooting. A forensics team arrived and I sat in the back seat of a cop car and shook a little. Most of the rest of the cops took off back on routine patrol to protect and serve. It was determined that my battered Taurus was still drivable and somebody pushed it into a small parking lot next to a building that professed to house a print shop. A cop locked it and handed over my keys.

I eventually was taken downtown to give a statement, get reports sorted out and tell my story again several times. Most of my physical reactions to the shooting had departed by the time Catherine showed up to claim me, much to the obvious envy of a few cops, and we went home.

Chapter 25

Later that evening, sitting on the couch wide awake, I wasn't much good for anything. The trembling had subsided, but I was still pretty nervy. In spite of what's found in novels and on television programs, cops don't engage in shootouts very often. PIs almost never. I couldn't remember the last time I shot at something other than a target at the range. The scotch in my drink helped. So did the calming, understanding, presence of my good friend, Catherine Mckerney.

She returned to my side on the living room couch after changing the CD in the stereo. The music filled the room and my head. Symphonic. *Something by Schumann*, I thought. "Do you want to talk about it," she said softly.

"No," I said, but then I did talk about it. "Killing is so irrevocable. It's so final. You can't step back from that edge, find another route. Once you've killed someone that door is closed."

"You sometimes tell me that even with a death, we are so good at finding information or clues, that no door is really closed."

"That's true, of course," I said. I laid my open hand on her thigh as if to reassure myself of her nearness. "But this guy leaves so many questions unanswered. We'll learn who he is and who he worked for. But why did he try to run me down last week, if it was even the same guy? And who was he working for then? How much did he get paid to take me out? Does he leave a family behind?"

"So many questions," Catherine murmured. "Did I tell you how very glad I am that we're here together right now and I'm not visiting you in a hospital. Or the morgue?"

We looked at each other. Then Catherine picked up the thread of our examination. "Will the answers to those questions help solve your cases?"

"Some of them might. One of the questions with possibly an important answer is how he knew where I was this afternoon. Did he follow me from the office? Or was he lying in wait? Did somebody at Murchison call him in to try to rub me out?"

I stopped and stared at the living room wall opposite. Then I stuck out my right hand and looked at the back. No tremors but my gut was still signaling me I was upset. A faint ache.

"Do you want another drink?"

"No, thanks. I'm as certain as I can be the truck was the same one that almost ran me down the other night downtown. That means I've been targeted for a while. I wish I could be sure it's related to the murder of Gottlieb."

"You seem pretty sure," Catherine said.

I looked up at her. She'd stepped into the kitchen to refresh her glass of wine.

"I'm not sure I get you."

"Ever since we got home and you've started talking about these cases, you've used the singular. You haven't referred to the cases, plural, as I just did. I think unconsciously your analytical brain has decided the murdered Gottlieb, the mysterious Ann/Anne and the missing Market woman are all connected."

I favored her with a long stare, recalling bits and pieces of our evening's talk. "Huh. I think you're right. And that means Gehrz is also part of it. Why didn't I see that?"

"Oh, you would have, I'm sure. Pretty sure. Just like I'm pretty sure you're almost convinced that Gottlieb, Gehrz, Ann/Anne, and Tiffany Market are all connected to something else." She smiled and sipped.

I understood this was serious and she wasn't laughing. "All right," I agreed. "Let's say for the moment, you're right." I paused and thought.

"We already know the Ann/Anne person says she saw Gottlieb murdered on the bridge."

"Why was she there, if she wasn't part of the murder?"

"Good question. My instinct says she's telling the truth and that the murder shook her up. At least, she's telling me some of the truth. I'm sure she's holding back something, and it has to do with why she was on the bridge."

"I think," Catherine said, "your Ann/Anne person is connected in some other way to the guy looking for his lady friend. What's his name again, Gehrz?"

"You do. Huh. Okay, let's run with that a minute. Ann/Anne shows up in my office and wants me to hustle the cops about Gottlieb, explaining she won't get involved. Gehrz shows up at about the same time looking for a woman named Market, at least so he says that's her name and he gives me pictures of the lady. At least one of which—the pictures—is doctored."

"I didn't know that."

I nodded and sipped my own drink. Then I lunged out of the sofa and started pacing. "Wait a minute. This Ann/Anne person insists she needs to remain in the background with me as her cut-out, and Gehrz is looking for a woman who faded into the background. Suppose for the moment Gehrz's inquiry is both camouflage and diversion?"

"I think you lost me. Please be careful with your drink. Put it down if you're going to wave your arms like that."

"I can't believe either Gehrz or Ann/Anne came to me out of the blue. Picked me out of the phone book. No way. Somebody knew about me and my connections to the cops."

"A leap in logic?" Catherine was always the more cautious.

"Wait. Let me test this. Gottlieb's murdered. Ann/Anne knows about it, why, because she's already hooked to him somehow. She didn't just 'happen' to be on the bridge that night. Now she wants the murderer caught, but she needs to stay out of the picture to protect others or maybe cover an investigation of some sort. Gehrz, also involved with Ann/Anne and Gottleib, approaches me to keep track of the woman's cover, to be sure she's secure. He feeds me a bogus search for his supposed girl friend, the Market woman. That takes time and alters my focus. Son of a bitch!" I don't like to be played, though I admit that playing games with clients, especially felons and other bad guys, is part of my stock in trade. In my DNA, some would say.

"I understand what you're saying. You think this Gehrz is using you to be sure the cover for Ann/Anne stays intact. That's because you have a stellar rep in town for finding lost folks, especially perpetrators of dark and illegal deeds."

"I love it when you use street talk," I smirked. "I bet that's the explanation for those two. That would mean I can stop looking for Tiffany Market, because she's Anne, or Ann is she. Her?

"And remember when that federal lawyer showed up the other day? I have a nagging suspicion Gehrz and the woman could be feds. Now I think it must be Gehrz, not that lawyer Madison, who sent me to that basement to get the package." I smirked with a degree of satisfaction. Hearing the words, gave the theory substance.

I sank back onto the couch. Even if I was right about those two, the attacks on me and the murder of Gottlieb still didn't connect tightly enough for my satisfaction. I needed to find some kind of rationale for that, some link. Was Murchison that connection?

The death of the truck driver earlier that day at my hand seemed extreme. Even though I'd been defending myself and I'd already been assured I wouldn't be prosecuted for the use of deadly force, the two unsuccessful attempts seemed over the top reactions to my messing about in the Gottlieb business. Maybe they weren't connected at all. But one of my early priorities was going to be squeezing Ann/Anne and Gehrz. There were still too many unanswered questions.

****

THE NEXT MORNING I WENT early to my office. It was one of those days. I hadn't slept well, my restlessness impelled Catherine to move to the guest bedroom at about three. The day was dark with low-hanging February cloud lumps. If there was a sun up there somewhere, I couldn't see it. I'd stopped for a Starbucks coffee on my way in and slopped some of it on the floor of my car, which didn't improve my mood. The cops let me pick it up, the car. The Taurus didn't drive quite right. No funny noises but the steering felt wrong. No big surprise there. Hell. I'd have to get it in the shop and rent something for the time being.

Two calls on my answering service were quickly disposed of and now I was staring at my office door, willing somebody to show up or one of my clients to call. Maybe I should call Ricardo and bug him about the Gottlieb affair.

While I thought about that briefly, I discovered I didn't have to call him because he was standing in the door to my office after barging noisily in from outside. I didn't recognize the man with him. A new partner?

"This is Sergeant Morris, a relatively new addition to Minneapolis team of investigators," Ricardo said. "We need to ask you some questions."

Morris was a large black man with a smooth, unmarked face and a serious expression. He had a pleasant baritone voice. We shook hands and sat down. His grip was firm but not crushing. I appreciated that.

Ricardo and I stared at each other for a moment. "You doin' okay?" he queried.

"I guess." I nodded once.

Ricardo extracted a sheaf of papers from a slender briefcase he was holding and laid a selection on the desk in front of me. It was an array of mug shots. Felons, I presumed.

"Recognize anyone?"

I switched on the desk lamp and stared at the pictures. "This guy looks familiar. I think I had a run-in with him a few years ago. I can't recall the details."

Ricardo nodded and I saw Morris scribbling in a small notebook he produced. "Try these." Simon slid another group of pictures in front of me.

"Here. This one. This is the guy driving the truck yesterday. Out by Murchison's." I tapped a picture and stared at the guy. Unremarkable, a typical police record picture, except I knew this guy was now dead by my hand.

Ricardo nodded and Morris made another note. "You told us about the incident with a box truck a few nights ago when you were on your way to Casey's. Can you say this was the same guy? Driving the truck?"

"No." I shook my head. "I never saw the driver of that truck. And I can't swear to it being the same truck, either. But both the one that hit me yesterday and the one the other night downtown were white box trucks with no markings. I'm almost certain they were the same truck."

Morris glanced at Ricardo Simon and said, "There have to be dozens of trucks like that in the metro."

Ricardo nodded. "I talked to the county attorney. Just to confirm that you aren't gonna be prosecuted and you can pick up your weapon any time after today."

"Thanks," I said. "Anything about this guy that would help understand why he came after me?"

Ricardo shrugged and glanced at Morris. "We know him. He has-had a record, including a short stint in Stillwater. A few violent incidents, mostly alcohol fueled. Muscle for hire, possibly. He's local so we'll be checking with relatives, the usual follow up, but we aren't likely to learn anything about why he came after you."

So he was not a contributing member of society. That knowledge didn't make me feel any better about having killed him.

We speculated a few minutes about why I'd been attacked. I didn't give the detectives anything useful in response to their probes. As they got up to leave, Ricardo revealed the real reason they'd come to my office for this interview.

"There have been inquiries," Ricardo said, struggling into his overcoat.

"Inquiries?"

"Yeah. The Chief has had questions asked about yourself."

"Really? From Saint Paul?"

Ricardo regarded me silently for a long moment. Both investigators were still.

"Saint Paul? Now why would you think that?"

"I dunno," I confessed. "It just popped into my head."

"Sure."

We both knew that Saint Paul officed state law enforcement people as well as federal agencies. People concerned with Homeland Security and who worked for some of the lettered organizations, like DEA and ATF and FBI and CIA.

Chapter 26

At four I prepared to leave the office for home, having accomplished just about nothing since Morris and Ricardo had departed. I figured to swing by the house in Roseville, stop at Byerly's to pick up a salmon steak for dinner, and then hie myself across the river to Kenwood. That was the plan.

The freakin' phone rang and instead of letting it go to the machine, I picked up. It was Ann/Anne and she sounded just a tad impatient.

"I guess you need to see me again, is that right?"

"Yes, ma'am. I require another deposit and while you're at it, bring me some more pages of that ledger, or whatever it is." Silence.

I almost decided she'd hung up when she said, "All right. But I can't come to your office."

"Okay. How 'bout you meet me in an hour in the restaurant attached to the Byerly's in Roseville. Do you know where the store is located? That work for you?"

"All right," she said again. Then she hung up. Apparently, she knew the area, or she'd find it.

Aha! The last time I talked with Mr. Gehrz, I'd let slip that another client of mine wasn't up to date on her retainer. I'd couched it in terms of appreciation for his—Gehrz's—prompt payments. Now, what kind of coincidence do you call it when you tell client A that client B is late and client B soon calls to set up a meet? I don't call it a coincidence at all. I call it trapping a client into revealing or confirming a connection. Also, the fact that she didn't have to ask for directions to the Byerly's store in question was some evidence that the woman was familiar with my neighborhood. Maybe more familiar than was comfortable.

I grabbed the phone and called a guy I knew in Roseville. "Wally," I said when he picked up. "I briefly need your talent in about an hour for just a couple of minutes. Can do?"

"Okay. What is it?"

Wally knows me. He's cautious.

"I'm gonna be in a booth in the restaurant in Byerly's in about fifty minutes. I need a nice sharp picture of the lady I'll be sitting with. It would be especially good if you can arrange it so I'm in the picture too."

"See you there," Wally said and hung up.

I left the office, smiling to myself. I was gonna get some serious mileage out of this meeting besides just another payment. Since I was early at the store I went to the meat counter and acquired a nice chunk of salmon for dinner later. As I was leaving the checkout and heading to the restaurant entrance off the next aisle, I saw a woman in a long white hooded coat coming into the restaurant from outside. Sparkles of fresh-fallen snow trembled on her shoulders. She disappeared into the women's bathroom and I went into the restaurant and secured a booth. I sat so I could see along the booths to the entrance. Moments later, the woman I knew as Ann/Anne appeared and slid into the seat across from me. The long white coat was not in evidence. She was wearing a nicely tailored gray suit and carrying a medium-sized good-quality leather shoulder bag. I wondered if she was armed. In my business I have these odd thoughts from time to time.

"Hello," I said. "Coffee or tea?"

We gave the waitress our order and my client produced an envelope. She opened it enough to show me its contents which consisted of some paper money and some other paper which I figured could be more pages from the ledger.

She laid the envelope on the table and put her hand on it. "I have to tell you, Mr. Sean. I'm disappointed with the progress of this case."

I raised my eyebrows in feigned surprise. "It's true the cops seem to be at a standstill and my contacts with a family member weren't very productive. But you didn't hire me to find the killer of Mr. Gottlieb. You just wanted a go-between, an interjector, as it were, between you and the police. Or so you said."

There was a flash of light from a corner of the restaurant and a quick burst of laughter. Somebody using a cell-phone camera, perhaps.

The woman stared at me. "Does that mean if I hire you to find and apprehend the killers, you'll work a little harder and charge me more money?"

"Not at all. That's because I wouldn't take the case. I don't take on murder cases. Oh, sure, in rare cases that I do accept, murder sometimes becomes a factor, but I try to leave homicide to our competent local police departments."

I never found out what she was going to say next because there was a loud crash in the aisle beside us when a man tripped over a bus boy carrying a loaded tray of dirty dishes. We both looked. Several people in booths around us stood up, or leaned out into the aisle to see what was happening, including Ann/Anne. She looked down at me, caught me watching her, instead of the mess of dishes on the floor. She shook her head slightly and slid the envelope to the middle of our table. Several staff rushed about cleaning up the mess and mopping spilled fluids, all the while apologizing to those of us in nearby booths.

"I think we're done here," Ann/Anne said softly. She took her hand off the envelope and slid out, then headed up the aisle, neatly sidestepping the bus boy. I didn't hear her say anything. I picked up the envelope she'd left and stuck it in my inside pocket. Then I finished my coffee. I'd hoped to detain her for a longer time, but even the best-laid plans and all that.

Fifteen minutes later I pulled into my driveway through a dusting of fresh snow. I saw the dark figure of a man waiting under one of my tall pines that grew beside the driveway as I left the car. Behind me there was only the tracks of a single vehicle in the street. Mine.

"Did you walk here from Byerly's?" I asked.

"Yep," said Wally. "It's not too cold and I need more exercise."

"There are no lights on in your house," I observed. "No tracks in the road, so I assume you crossed the lots from Fairview. Came in the shorter, back way."

"Correct. Kept me off the street."

"Any particular reason for all this caution?" I didn't ask Wally if he got the picture I wanted. He's a competent professional.

"We need to go back to the restaurant."

"Why is that?"

"To get your picture. I left it with my cousin who works in the kitchen."

"Okay. How did that come to pass?" On the way Wally explained that he happened to observe the woman I met approaching the entrance from the parking area. She was wearing a long white coat with the hood thrown back and he said he thought she was attractive. He also noticed a man walking with the woman. Because he had a good view of her through the window from inside the restaurant, he recognized her when she came to my booth.

"See, I was carrying two cameras. I only got the one shot when the bin of dishes fell over, and I gave that camera to Don, my cousin, to hold while

I grabbed some more shots with the other camera. Then I went outside and the guy who was with your client found me. He took my camera."

"He what?"

"He smacked into me. I wasn't watching where I was going and we tangled and fell. It's slippery out, 'case you hadn't noticed. I dropped it. The camera. A car was coming. I rolled out of the street and when I got back up, the guy was gone and I couldn't find the camera."

"Did you see him take the camera?"

"No, and it's dark, but I'm sure he did."

"But the picture I want is on the camera that Don, your cousin, has?"

"On both. I had one in each hand and fired at the same time. I wanted to be sure to get at least one good one and usually when I do these shoots for you there isn't time to reshoot or wait for the flash to recharge."

"I didn't notice a flash."

Wally grinned in the dim light from the dash and said, "After you explained what you wanted me to do, I called Don. He suggested dropping a tray of dishes."

"I'll cover the cost of the breakage," I said, "and the lost camera."

"No problem," Wally said.

By now we'd reached the Byerly's parking lot and I paused at the entrance so Wally could retrieve his camera from his cousin. I waited in the car, scanning the immediate area. Wally came back out and slid into my car, pressing buttons on the back of his expensive Nikon SLR. Then he showed me the screen. There we were in living color, my almost profile and Ann/Anne in an easily identifiable three-quarter shot. She was half-out of her seat and I was looking at her, one might even suggest with adoration on my face. Dandy.

"It's lucky you used two cameras," I said as we drove away.

"Yeah, if the guy looks at the images on the card he got he'll assume he got the only picture of her. And it just happens that it wasn't this camera I held onto, but the little point and shoot."

"Yeah," I agreed, but I silently wondered as we drove home through the snowy night. The thing was getting more problematical. I hadn't considered Tiffany Market might have an escort and I should have. Maybe the fat envelope she'd left me would provide some answers.

Chapter 27

How and where had my blond benefactor, my client, acquired the ledger pages she was feeding me? I still hadn't figured that out but I was happy to discover a bunch of them in the fat envelope that same client, Ann/Anne, had left on the dining booth table at Byerly's.

I copied them, along with the color eight-by-ten Wally supplied a few hours later. The next day I made several smaller color copies, cropping my own face out of the shot. What I planned to do was to heat up the hunt for the lady, Ann/Anne, or perhaps Tiffany. I was almost certain in my mind that the two women were one and the same. I was also pretty sure the ledger pages she was feeding me were the reason Manfred Gottlieb had been murdered. I was confident, but a little less certain, that my client had acquired the ledger in an extralegal way. Maybe she stole it from Gottleib. Maybe he gave it to her. Nah, unlikely.

Repackaging the fresh ledger pages and mailing copies to my friend in the Language Department at Macalester College took some time and brought no fresh insights. My friend at Mac had translated other materials for me. I knew he'd be discreet and while he almost always asked questions about the material, he wasn't persistent when I demurred. I assumed he knew I'd lied to him on a few past occasions.

Now that I had a decent picture of my client, I was going to retrace some of my steps. I took the pictures and went off to do my thing. Initially, I left some copies for the Minneapolis cops I knew would have some level of interest in keeping eyes peeled for the woman.

The scenario I was building went like this: Appear in a medium-sized city where you have no relatives or other above-the-line associations. Why? I'm leaving that alone for the moment, I told myself. Find a temporary residence in a downtown hotel. Apply for a bunch of jobs, starting with a temp position that could and did, lead to something permanent. With a job one gets to give an apartment leasing agent a reference.

Leasing agent calls Human Resources, which verifies the woman has a job. Fine, lease is signed, woman, named Tiffany Market, moves in some time later. The apartment in question is centrally located in Northeast Minneapolis, not too close and not too far, it turns out, from any of the players in my little drama. No one pays a whole lot of attention to that, or to her comings and goings. Fine.

I'm in my car, driving to the Ford place in Roseville where I'll surrender my Taurus to the tender mercies of the body shop and rent something suitable. Maybe they'll have a new Lincoln stretch limo. Right. With that business taken care of, the shop mechanic will call with repair costs and the timeline. I'm now renting a black 2011 Ford Taurus. It's a four-door with most of the bells and whistles, but not all. It doesn't have the souped-up engine, nor is there a handgun bracket beneath the dash, or the cleverly concealed space in the trunk where I can stash special supplies when I need to. Driving around town with a bag of tools designed to clandestinely enter places with a minimum of breakage, or with a sawed off shotgun, let's say, would lead to arrest and detainment, should I be involved in a casual fender-bender or a traffic survey stop. Better such things be transported, when rarely required, in secure and secret places. I decided to return to the woman's apartment building for another examination. Yes, I'd been there before but sometimes, reexamination after a little time has passed can bring fresh insight. It was worth a shot.

I stopped in a no-parking zone in front of Tiffany Market's apartment building. Through a time-honored subterfuge, I gained entrance to the building and hot-footed it up the stairs to the fourth floor. In the stairwell, which is roomy and well appointed, I turned and stared for a moment out the glass wall at the city of Minneapolis. Off to my left, through the bare tree branches was the graceful curve of Jimmy Hill's Stone Arch Bridge over the Mississippi River. It was the bridge that once carried Mr. Hill's railroad tracks to the west. It was the same bridge from which person or persons unknown, threw the unfortunate Mr. Gottlieb to his death one cold snow-filled February night.

I walked quietly to the door which I believed to be the entrance to Ms. Market's apartment. I didn't knock. I didn't want to advertise my presence, and, besides, I didn't believe anybody would answer my knock. Since the hall was empty I stood a few paces away and carefully examined the door and the door frame. I was pretty sure I saw where a tiny wide-angle camera lens might have been placed to surveil the immediate vicinity of the door.

Now, I could easily understand a hole in the door with a little lens to give a wide view. Anybody in an apartment building would want that, even if the building was locked or had some sort of security system. But a camera?

Seemed excessive, if that's what it was. Another odd thing to add to my list of oddities about this woman.

I went to the office of the complex and talked to the receptionist. I watched her closely when I showed her the picture of Tiffany Market. She allowed as how the woman looked "vaguely familiar," but she wouldn't identify her absolutely. She did recall having thought she occasionally saw a tenant wearing a long white overcoat with a fur-lined hood. She also explained it wasn't the policy of the owners of the complex to talk about their tenants. Respect for privacy. It wasn't much of an identification, but it added to my file.

When I got to Target Central I was able to grab a few minutes with a woman who worked in HR—Human Resources. She allowed as how she recognized Tiffany Market in the picture. Not new information, just confirmation. I always liked it when I got similar or identical answers from different sources.

Since there had been some inquires from across the river, according to my friend Ricardo Simon, I took myself across the frozen Mississippi to St. Paul, to a large imposing stone office building in the middle of downtown known as the Federal Building.

There, after some security scanning, I was allowed to enter an ordinary office on the top floor with a discreet plaque that identified it as Homeland Security. I was asked to wait for a little while after I explained my mission. The man who introduced himself as an agent led me to a small nondescript conference room. He was as bland and ordinary-looking as could be. That is to say he looked like any other mid-level professional one might encounter walking on the street in downtown Saint Paul of a summer noon. He had one head, two arms, two legs and was fully dressed in a nice-fitting suit. The suit was brown and so was his hair, a neatly trimmed cut. His shirt was tan and his tie was appropriate. I don't think he said his name was Mr. Brown.

He smiled and seemed friendly, but he told me just about nothing. His answers to my queries were that he didn't know, couldn't say or wasn't prepared to give a definitive answer. He did agree that were I presently or in the future to become the subject of scrutiny by any legally appropriate agency of the United States government, it would be for cause.

In other words, if I did something suspicious or intersected with someone already under investigation, there might be a file on me somewhere.

"Is there such a file?" I asked

"That would fall under classified information," he replied.

"I can request my files under the Freedom of Information Act, can I not?"

"Correct. Every citizen has the right to request access to whatever information the government may have on themselves."

What he didn't say was that such requests have a habit of taking an extremely long time to be filled. Understaffed agencies, I assume, owing to budget limitations.

"Are you aware that I was visited by a Justice Department attorney recently?"

"I can't say," my agent responded. "Do you happen to know which department he represented?"

"Yes," I said. "He produced identification that said he worked for OSI, the Office of Special Investigations."

That got a small reaction. Mr. Brown Suit of Homeland Security had heard of that office and knew what it meant. I dropped some other names, Gehrz, Gottlieb, Madison, Murchison, and Market just to see what the reaction might be. Nada, almost nothing. So I thanked the man and left the office. I was only a little wiser than before. I felt certain that I was likely to have similar conversations with representatives of the other alphabets. So I tested my theory with the local FBI office. They wouldn't tell me, of course, if I was the target of an active investigation, but, yes, my name was in their files, inevitably because of my occasional contacts with persons of interest to the Bureau. But that was all they were prepared to say.

I was satisfied. Sort of. At least I was a little wiser. What I now was able to surmise with a reasonably high degree of accuracy was that all these people were linked. Gehrz, the woman, Ann/Anne who was most certainly also known as Tiffany Market, the unfortunate Gottlieb, attorney Derrol Madison and his repatriation group Atria, and the Murchison manufacturing family. It wasn't that Homeland Security or the FBI had anything hot going with me or my associates in this case, but by talking to these agencies I was able to confirm in my own mind my assumptions as to this being a single case. I would proceed on those assumptions, but what I now needed was a better connection of all this to the Murchisons.

I also needed to figure out what, exactly, I had detected regarding Gehrz and the Market woman and the federales.

Chapter 28

My office answering machine indicated that I had several calls so I sat down to process them. The first two were calls from sales people trying to interest me in some kind of new fangled surveillance gear. In both cases I declined to schedule an interview or a demonstration, mainly because I rarely used such equipment and I wasn't adept at setting up or operating it. I didn't even have much interest in learning about such gear. If I decided I needed that kind of help, there were people I could call on, people who made it their business to learn and operate such equipment, experts. I was an expert in my own little realm, just not that one.

The other reason I rejected their entreaties was a vague feeling that there was something a little off about both callers. I didn't think the suggested use of their gear was wholly legal. Was this an attempt to set me up? To catch me in something that might result in jail and loss of my license? Or was my paranoia antenna just a little more sensitive these days?

Mr. Gehrz called me. I offered to set up a meeting to give him a final report.

"Final report, Mr. Sean?"

The line buzzed in my ear and the man's voice faded in and out.

"Yeah. I found your Tiffany Market. In fact, I had a brief meeting with her late yesterday afternoon."

"Did you indeed."

"That's right. I'm happy to report she's just fine. I've surveiled the address you gave me and confirmed that she is or was living there and that she did in fact work briefly for Target Corporation. I know a couple of other things." I paused to learn if I'd get a reaction.

"She's alive then. You're sure."

I was tempted right then to offer him a recent picture of her. I considered that and thought about offering to meet him at the same Byerly's restaurant where the picture had been made, just to tweak him a little. I refrained. I didn't have a secure enough handle on this whole thing to indulge in a tweak without anticipating just how the tweakee would react. But I'd figure out a way, because I was still pissed at him for manipulating me, even knowing that he was still at it. Anyway, I was sure he had a recent picture. If I asked him to return the camera he'd snatched so I wouldn't have to buy Wally a new one, that would be another tweak. So I didn't ask.

There was a pause and electronics buzzed some more. That was odd and I wondered if Gehrz was using some kind of screening or recording device.

"Do I owe you some additional recompense?"

"No. If you'd like, I'll be happy to provide a detailed written account of my expenses. You wouldn't even have to come here. I could mail it to you."

"That won't be necessary. I'm greatly relieved to learn Ms. Market is all right, which is all I asked of you."

"Mmm. I had the impression when she and I last talked that she'll be in touch with you shortly. I think that should relieve your mind."

"I see. Thank you. Have a good day."

We disconnected and I unplugged the little digital recorder I had activated as soon as I heard his voice. I copied the file to another, newer, digital voice recorder and put that one in a padded envelope which I addressed to one of my aforementioned experts and dropped it in the mail. My friend would examine, dissect, and extract all sorts of possibly useful information. Or not. I habitually recorded my phone conversations and like this one, most were of little or no use. But I made them anyway.

The original recording I left on the machine and stowed the recorder in its usual place in my desk. I assumed Gehrz had recorded all our conversations at his end, but there was a chance he'd decide to compare his with mine, just for the sake of accuracy. Yeah, right.

Meanwhile I reexamined my meeting with Ms. Target. I probably should have suggested to her that she get in touch with her swain, if that's what he was. To do that, while we were at Byerly's, would have required me to reveal more of my suspicions about the links between Ann/Anne/Tiffany and Mr. Gehrz. I wasn't prepared to do that just yet. Knowing something about your adversary, and I was coming to the belief that Gehrz and I were adversaries, can be advantageous.

I pulled out my file on Gottlieb and added a scribbled note that could mean anything, depending on your paranoia or exposure to legal procedures. It said, Gottlieb-Madison-Atria-Radzyn. I added in block print the word TRACE.

I decided to do some research into what might be the genesis of this whole convoluted case. I had some sketchy information from Aaron about his family roots so I went off to my neighborhood library for some assistance.

Several hours later, with the help of a pleasant and patient librarian I had learned a good deal about a family named Gottlieb, from Radzyn, Poland. Since I was not in the genealogy business. I wasn't interested in heavy validation, but I had a pile of notes that should interest both Aaron and the police and might just reveal the root cause of the case.

I took my notes and myself home to Kenwood and spread my stuff out on the table in Catherine's extra bedroom which was now an office and housed her big computer and some exercise gear I tried to avoid looking at.

The telephone in my office rang. I picked up. It was Aaron Gottlieb calling from Chicago and he was pretty excited. "I found something interesting," he said.

"Good," I said. "What is it?"

"Well, I had most of the stuff from the Minneapolis house that was saved shipped here, remember?"

"Ah," I said. Actually, I was pretty sure he hadn't told me that, but I didn't think it mattered. "And?"

"I'm donating a lot of it to places like Goodwill and the Salvation Army, you know?"

"Yes," I said.

"So some friends were packing up the boxes, including a lot of books which weren't damaged. Well, they smell smoky, some of them."

"Okay," I said. I kept the receiver to my ear and rolled my chair down the short hall to the kitchen where I snagged a bottle of Fat Tire out of the fridge.

"Anyway the other day one of the kids found something in the pages of a dictionary, I think it was. Receipts. Or bills of sale." His words were becoming a river of sound.

"Easy, Aaron, slow down. Take a breath."

"Okay, thanks, Mr. Sean. Anyway they're in German, I think, but some of it's in Polish. There were four pages in all. It's a listing of goods, like furniture and clothes and other stuff like kitchen utensils. I made some copies and I just got a partial translation back."

I remembered my conversation with Madison and the group tracing stolen goods from occupied countries in World War II. "Aaron," I said sharply, breaking into his train of words. "I think I need to see that list. Send me a copy as fast as you can."

"Oh, sure. Do you think it has anything to do with my uncle's murder?"

"No way to tell until I can examine the documents. Send it overnight express to my address." I gave him Catherine's address because I knew a large envelope would be under lock and key downstairs until I could retrieve it. My mailbox in Roseville was at the curb and my office wasn't much better.

"Aaron, be sure to put the original somewhere safe, like with your lawyer or maybe in an office safe. It could be very valuable."

We rang off, as some Brits were wont to say and I went back to contemplating the materials I had before me.

Radzyn was a small city on the Bug River about seventy-five miles east of Warsaw, near the international boundary with the Soviet Union. The Gottliebs had apparently lived in the area or the town itself for generations until the pestilence that was called Nazism overran the country. Of Manfred Gottlieb and his immediate family I had found precious little information. What I did know was mostly inferences I could draw from collections of anecdotal narratives by members of the community before, during and after the war. And there were a few family memories Aaron had dredged up and provided.

His ancestors had been reasonably well off and lived in a fairly substantial home, what we might call upper middle class. They were educated and appreciated cultural efforts by others. There were, according to Aaron, who got the information in bits and pieces from his great uncle Manfred, a few significant pictures on the walls of the home.

When Manny went back to Radzyn, he'd been recently liberated from a concentration camp. Before that he'd survived successive invasions by Soviet and then German regular army troops. Those troops were ultimately replaced by the Gestapo, and then the town was liberated by another wave of Soviet troops. He found the family house almost destroyed.

A small unit of American troops were deployed at the edge of town. It was apparently this unit to which old man Albert Murchison had been assigned. I couldn't prove it, but I knew the American and Soviet troops were all over the place.

All well and good, but where did it get me? Not very far toward identifying the killer of Manfred Gottlieb, except for a couple of possible facts.

In the early middle years of the twentieth century, a painter came through Gottlieb's town. He did a few portraits of important people and the stories were that he also produced a few landscapes. His name was Abraham Neumann. In later times, some of his paintings had gained a measure of attention in the art world. I decided that although I was far from being any kind of art connoisseur, I had better take a look at the painting that had been donated to the Institute by Al Murchison.

Chapter 29

The next day I found my way to South Minneapolis where after a brief inquiry I entered a long, high-ceilinged gallery. Off the gallery on one side was an entrance to a much smaller though still sizeable space and there, reverently displayed on one wall, was a single painting. An oil painting it was, a nice pastoral scene of meadows divided by a meandering stream between grass-thick banks. It was not large. There were no people or animals in the scene, but way in the distance on one side were daubs of paint signifying buildings of some sort. A village perhaps.

Affixed to the wall was some information of the usual kind, identifying what those in the art world call the provenance, or ownership of the work. The legend stated that the work had been donated to the Institute by a present member of the board of trustees, one Albert M. Murchison. Interesting, to me, was the phrase, "Attributed to Abraham Neumann." I learned years earlier that such a phrase usually meant the statement wasn't ironclad or rock solid.

I sat down, alone, on the long bench before the painting and regarded it in silence. It was the kind of art that seemed to generate a feeling of peace and well-being among viewers. After a while I got up and leaned in close to the surface of the painting, peering at the lower edges. In one corner, sure enough, I found a signature that was almost indecipherable. But if I stared at it hard enough I convinced myself it said A. Neumann.

I went back and sat down and thought about it. I was thinking about what it must have been like in that small far-off town at the end of the war. Soviet and American troops wandering about, doing whatever they were assigned to. Residents and former residents would be trying to find almost obliterated streets and avenues and homes and businesses. Apparently many if not all the homes and shops in the town had been indiscriminately destroyed during the successive invasions. Manfred Gottlieb arrived home after what must have been an arduous journey from the concentration camp, to find almost nothing of his home or family. So what Mr. Gottlieb did was to pack up everything he could find of any sort of value, personal or intrinsic, and shipped himself and his belongings off to America. I'd seen what he brought back, the big cabinet in the attic, packed with an odd assortment of stuff, and the books. I was deep into my contemplation, something I normally didn't do in a public place because of the assorted bad guys who might be looking to beat on me for imagined wrongs.

I realized someone else had come into the small gallery and was approaching from behind. I tensed my thighs in case I had to move suddenly. Then she sat down beside me. Not close, you understand, but on the same bench. When I glanced over, I discovered Ursula Skranslund had joined me.

"Hello, Ursula," I said softly.

"Hello, Mr. Sean," she said back.

"How is it that we meet here, today?"

"Mr. Gottlieb told me about this painting. He said it was of a scene near his home. In Poland."

"Did he tell you anything else about it?"

Ursula shook her head. "No. I just started coming here to see it after he died and the house burned. He was like a grandfather to me, you know? I miss him."

I nodded. I decided not to tell her of my suspicions that the painting might be the reason Mr. Gottlieb had been murdered. I got up to leave and smiled at her. "I have to go now, but I expect to come back to see the painting again. Take care."

She smiled sadly and nodded. Then she turned to look at the painting of the Bug River. I went to find a telephone.

Pay phones were becoming a rare breed in this town. It looked like I was destined to pop for a cell phone sometime soon. Eventually I located a phone in the lobby of a small motel across the street from the museum and reached out to my friends down the hall from my office. The thing rang twice in my ear and Belinda picked up. "Yeah?"

"Is this hacker heaven?" I enquired. "Establishment of the beauteous Revulons, Betsy, and Belinda?"

"Knock it off, Sean, or I'll put you on hold. Whaddyouwant?"

"Research request, my pet. Last year, a man named Albert Murchison donated a painting to MIA. The painting is a landscape, attributed to a Polish artist named Abraham Neumann. It purports to be a scene along the Bug River in Poland, naturally."

"Okay. What am I looking for?"

"Dunno, exactly, so that must mean everything. Especially provenance."

"You got anything else?"

"I suspect it was painted in the 1920s. No later than 1935. Oh, and it was probably collateral in a bank loan Al Murchison took out around 1945 to finance the purchase of a machine shop in north Minneapolis."

"Intriguing. Haven't we been over this ground?"

"Yes."

"I'll jump right on it," she said.

Belinda, being a large well-endowed woman, with copious waves of bright blond hair, the vision that came to mind of jumping on anything was not one I cared to share. I hung up the receiver.

More library research seemed appropriate. I wanted to acquire more background about the Murchison family. Facing Hennepin Avenue in downtown Minneapolis was a nice new central library. On my way to the library, I ruminated about meeting Ursula at MIA. What were the chances of that? I'm always suspicious of coincidence, even while recognizing that it does happen. Frequently. Had she been following me? Was she really so attached to the dead Gottlieb that she had a psychological need to visit the painting more than once?

My gut told me to pay attention but not to worry unduly. I continued to the library.

There, with help from the staff, I acquired notes on the Murchisons. The information was illuminating. I started with some census information from 1900. No Murchisons. They showed up in 1910, a man and a wife. Laborer, it said. I knew if I widened the search, I might learn where Mr. Albert Murchison had emigrated from but at the moment I didn't care.

On I went until by 1920 there were several family members. The family had a disturbing tendency to name male children Albert. I lost the generational thread a few times. But eventually, I was able to pinpoint one Albert Malcolm Murchison who joined the Army of these United States in 1939. He was eighteen at the time. Seven years later, one year before the end of his second hitch, in 1946, Mr. Albert Malcolm Murchison, having attained the enlisted rank of master sergeant, was mustered out and returned to the bosom of his family. Along the way he'd acquired a wife and two sons.

Then he and his father went to a bank in Northeast Minneapolis and floated a loan, a sufficiently large enough loan to allow them to purchase a smallish machine shop, which they renamed Murchison Manufacturing.

I was looking at a locally produced neighborhood history a kindly librarian had located for me. The entry was short and not terribly informative.

It was at that moment I realized that my growing itch was real. Somebody was watching me. I closed the book and rose, leaving my coat over the chair and wandered casually to a nearby water fountain. I drank, peering beneath my arm. Then I stood and pivoted so I could sweep the whole room. It was large and there were a half-dozen people scattered about. My radar continued to itch, but I couldn't detect anyone who seemed interested in myself. I went back to my table, put on my coat and went down the escalator to the street level, where I exited toward the parking lot. I wondered if my friendly hacker had been successful. A tall man in a bulky and long dark overcoat wearing an old-fashioned black fedora pulled low over his forehead followed me out of the library and into the parking lot.

Chapter 30

Back in my cozy little office in Northeastern Minneapolis, I was pleased to be reminded that the owner of the building was generous with winter heat, if not electric lighting in the halls. Every so often I would wonder how much potential business I and the other tenants lost because the hall lighting was so dim. On the other hand...

The light on my recently acquired answering machine was blinking. There was a single call and a lot of static or white noise. The calls from Ann/Anne and Mr. Gehrz were no longer in evidence. The single call had been recorded an hour ago while I was at MIA contemplating the Bug River banks as interpreted by Mr. Neumann, and conversing with Ms. Skransland.

I crawled around my office and examined the locks and the outer door. I could see no evidence of the lock being forced. There wasn't enough dust on the floor to leave traces so whoever had cleaned up had been careful. For that I was grateful. One of the private investigator's expenses is the repair of office equipment and doors, due to forcible entries from time to time.

I considered my files which had not been removed although there was some evidence the copy machine may have been used. I didn't get the point. Removing voice evidence might derail a poorly put together court case, but surely the Market/Gehrz operatives calculated that I must have copies of crucial information stashed somewhere else. Or, maybe I didn't.

The single telephone message was from Belinda Revulon, informing me she had some interesting material for me. I replaced the receiver in its cradle and went down the hall. The lights were on but nobody answered my knock. I considered my options for a moment when Betsy Revulon appeared from the direction of the bathrooms.

"Hang on," she called. "Belinda had to go see a client in St. Louis Park so she gave me your stuff."

We went into the two-room suite crowded with electronic equipment. The equipment had uses I couldn't discern or even imagine. There were a couple of open metal racks loaded with gear that sported lights and wires and connectors and displayed brand names like Motorola, IBM, Apple, and so on.

Betsy snagged a file folder from a table and turned to me. "Everything we found so far is in here. We think you should go over this and then maybe we can narrow the search, if you need us to. Turns out there are a ton of Murchisons all over the country. I suspect you'll be most interested in what we've turned up on one Alvin M. Murchison whose son Clem is the Murchison you talked to the day of your attempted assassination." She gave me a small smirk.

"I can take this material back to my office?"

"Most definitely. We printed everything out. The data is stored elsewhere. I do want to call your attention to a PDF photograph we collected." She riffled through the pages and fished out a single sheet. The picture was a blurry copy of a newspaper photo and story about the good things in the community being done by a local bank. The line at the top of the clipping said it was from a northeast neighborhood newspaper, probably a weekly. The date was April something, 1955. The accompanying picture showed a smiling, young and portly gentleman sitting in a high-backed chair behind an impressive desk. The caption said the picture showed the civic-minded president of the bank, one Charles Carter.

"Look at the wall behind the guy," Betsy said.

"Ah, yes," I said. There was a painting hanging on the wall. The picture had been cropped so we couldn't see the whole painting but I recognized it right off. "There's the Neumann painting. No way there could be two so similar paintings in Minneapolis." I smiled at Belinda. "Great. And thanks."

"Yep," she nodded. "I recognized it from your description."

I took myself and my new evidence linking the parties together to my office.

I nipped down to the store in the corner of our building. I believe in a bygone era it was called a sundry store. I almost never patronized the place. The owner carried a limited variety of pre-packaged sandwiches. This day I felt pressed for time so I grabbed what was labeled a cheese on rye and a can of diet cola from the cooler. Then I beat it back upstairs to my office.

My case, I realized had essentially disappeared. Ann/Anne, who was really Tiffany Market, had been found. Therefore, Mr. Gehrz was out of the picture, since my mandate from him was to find the woman and assure myself that she was in good health. I'd done that.

Her entreaty to me was being followed in that I supplied all I knew about the murder to the cops. If they wanted to interview her, it was up to them to locate her. Or it was up to her to come forward, an action I'd suggested to her more than once. That she'd so far refused wasn't my problem either.

I had no dog in the hunt for the killer of Manny Gottlieb. Aaron hadn't hired me, nor had Derrol Madison. They were both involved, but I wasn't sure to what level. I could close the files on this business except for a couple of things.

Murchison. A possibly purloined painting. Somebody wanted my head. That somebody had tried for me twice. I didn't believe for a New York minute that the guy I'd had to kill outside the Murchison Manufacturing plant was acting on his own. Nor did I believe his removal from the scene had ended the threat. No, there was something else going on here.

Having satisfied my own belief that I couldn't yet close the book, I decided on my next step.

I would talk to a certain ex-banker in Nordeast.

The research my lovelies down the hall had supplied me with not only provided the name of the bank, Northeastern State Bank of Minneapolis, and its street address, but also the name of the current president. There was also a few lines indicating that the most recent former president, although retired, still maintained a small office in the building.

He was my next target. I was going into Northeast Minneapolis to talk with a banker.

His name was Carter, Charles Carter, I was informed by the petite receptionist in the neat lobby. Of course I already knew that.

I could have called to make an appointment, but I often find that showing up unexpectedly can elicit the kind of information I really want. That assumes one's target is available. Chuck Carter could have been in Florida or on a warm beach in the South Seas. He wasn't. He was in his office in Minneapolis and if I'd take a seat, she was sure Mr. Carter would be able to spare a few minutes to talk with a graduate student in banking from an obscure Western college she'd never heard of. That would be me.

I smiled, sat and perused a business magazine of some sort.

Ten minutes later, a slender, white-haired, nicely set up gentleman in an extremely well-tailored pinstripe suit met me at the door to his office. His smile displayed a mouthful of very white and straight teeth. His face was seamed and darkly tanned, as if he spent a lot of time these days on a golf course, and if his age had stooped him a little, his handshake was firm. He appeared truly glad to see me.

For the first few minutes we danced around the little fibs I'd told to get into Charles Carter's office. About being a graduate student from out of town researching influential community banks. About not knowing much of anything about Nordeast Minneapolis. After a few minutes, Carter began to suspect I had other motives because he held up one arthritic hand and said, "Mr. Sean, just what is it you think I can do for you?"

"Thank you," I said. "You can search your memory for the circumstances surrounding a loan you approved back in 1946, a loan made to a local man named Albert Murchison."

Carter raised his eyebrows. There seemed to be a good deal of that going around, these days.

"In those days, we still had loan committees," he said

"True, sir, but applications started with employees of the bank, correct? And in this particular case, because the loan was, I imagine, fairly substantial, I'm betting Murchison came directly to you, the president of his local bank."

"Albert Murchison. I remember him. A veteran of the war, recently back from Europe and looking to make something of himself."

"That's the man. Now, while you recollect, I want to tell you what I know about that meeting. I don't expect you to reveal private matters, but it would help me enormously if you'd indicate where I might have false information." Carter nodded and seemed to relax. He wasn't going to be grilled about something questionable. I didn't actually have any questionable information. He wouldn't know that, of course, unless he'd made a few questionable deals.

So I related Murchison's war record and his immediate job seeking actions after he was discharged.

"And then he showed up in your office asking about a loan. He wanted to buy or buy into a small manufacturing shop just a few blocks away from us, as it happens. He wanted a fairly sizeable loan, several tens of thousands, I expect and you must have been doubtful at first. But then he produced a surprise. He had somehow acquired a painting, a landscape by a man named Abraham Neumann. When you saw it, you allowed as how you could approve the loan with the painting as part of the collateral. And apparently, Mr. Murchison agreed to let you hold the painting. I see by your expression, Mr. Carter, you are with me here.

"But then, after the loan went through and you took possession of the painting, you did something a little unusual."

I slid a photograph out of my slender briefcase, the one I held on my lap, and laid it on the desk between us. It was a copy of the eight-by-ten black and white newspaper picture from a celebration in Northeast Minneapolis. I didn't much care what the occasion was, but there were a couple of people in the picture with Mr. Carter, in his office at the time. Nineteen sixty or around then. And on the wall behind them was the Neumann landscape. It was only partially in the photo's frame, but enough to clearly identify it as the same picture now hanging in state at the Minneapolis Institute of Art.

"Instead of just storing the painting, you had it framed and hung on the wall of your office."

I slid the photograph closer to Mr. Carter. He looked at it and a big smile creased his wrinkles.

"Oh, yes, I remember that day well. The bank was participating in a neighborhood holiday."

"Now, it gets less exact," I went on while he looked at the photo. "Some years later, Mr. Murchison came to you and paid off the loan, and took possession of the painting. His collateral, correct? And sometime after that, maybe a few years later, you began to think about that painting. Maybe you read a story about how the Nazis had plundered many art collections all over Europe and how some members of liberating armies did similar things. GIs and others were collecting the odd bits to bring home as souvenirs.

"But that painting was too fine to just be a casual souvenir wasn't it? Even though it wasn't highly valued, your bank had loaned a substantial piece of change for that painting hadn't you? You even liked the painting well enough to hang it in your office and allow it to be photographed, right?

"But then a sour note or two was raised. I think you talked to Al Murchison, now an influential member of the community with a successful manufacturing company. You talked to him about the painting and between you, decided the better part of valor was to get rid of it. Due to some changes in attitudes here and there, that painting was beginning to look like a liability, am I right?"

I smiled at Charles Carter. My teeth were showing. He was still looking down at the photograph.

"You wanted him to get rid of the painting quietly, right? But he went against your wishes, right? Making a donation to MIA was a public splash. I suppose Mr. Murchison decided a donation of the work would give him a nice extra benefit in the form of public approbation and a tax write-off. Then

MIA decided they'd better test the provenance of the thing because they sure didn't want a stolen painting in their collection, did they? No more did you. Especially a painting that probably had been feloniously liberated in Eastern Poland."

My voice was rising a little as my anger grew. I knew Carter wasn't responsible for the theft, his crime was passivity. What he knew or thought wasn't important to him. As soon as he began to suspect that Murchison hadn't come by the painting legitimately, he should have spoken up, persuaded Murchison to take the piece to the authorities. Had they done that, Manny Gottlieb might still be alive. A stretch? Perhaps.

I didn't think Chuckie Carter, former bank president, had ordered Gottlieb killed, nor had he tried to have me gunned down. But he was partially responsible for two untimely deaths.

I stopped talking abruptly and sat there wishing I had a glass of cool water. Carter said nothing for a long silent moment. Then he sighed noisily.

"It was all a long time ago," he muttered.

"Well, that's not quite true," I said. "I think you know or suspect that some member of the Murchison clan is responsible for Mr. Gottlieb's death. What's more, I won't be the least bit surprised if we discover you know about the two attempts on my life. You're a smart man, Mr. Carter. You can put two and two together, just as I can."

Carter's reaction was unexpected. He hadn't made the connections or he didn't know about the shootout in the intersection three blocks away. I was hoping he'd make some waves with one of the Murchison's which would quite possibly provoke a revealing response. His mouth fell open and he stared at me, white-faced. For a moment, I thought he was having a heart attack, but then he recovered and shook his head. I watched his face close up and I knew the interview was over.

I got up to leave, abruptly shoving back my chair. The feet made a growling kind of sound on the wooden floor. Carter was still looking at the photograph when I said goodbye and stalked out of the bank. I left the copy of the photograph. I had others.

On my way through the lobby, I noticed a tall, gaunt, man leaning over one of the counters writing on a scrap of paper. I thought he looked vaguely familiar, then I forgot about him.

Chapter 31

I drove back to our Kenwood apartment. I realized along the way I'd let my anger influence the way I handled my interview with ex-bank president Carter. Not good. Riding up in the elevator from the garage to our floor I realized something else.

I hadn't paid my usual attention to my changing surroundings on the drive to Kenwood. I'd been on automatic pilot, not a good place to be when somebody had already taken a couple of runs at me. There was something else as well. I knew the guy in the bank lobby had been vaguely familiar. I thought now it might have been the same guy who was at the entrance to the library the other day. Obviously, I needed to sharpen my best practices and also find out if I was right about that fellow. Was I being followed? And if so, why? By whom?

I let myself into our place and checked my gat into the safe in the spare bedroom-cum-office. It was a measure of respect and trust that Catherine had given me the combination to the safe. It was also true that she didn't like having my gats lying about, either. I whipped together a light scotch and ice and sat down to read over the notes and information the Revulon cousins had cobbled together for me. I hoped to find some nuggets requiring a little more concentrated mining that could prove fruitful.

My mind didn't let me focus on the latest sheet of paper. After a few minutes of staring at the page, I hadn't actually read the words. Crap. I closed the file and went to pick up the large bundle of copies. Since Catherine and I were acting like a married couple, and cohabiting two residences, I had files in the office we shared. What? I may be still in the twentieth century as it regards a lot of electronic advances, but I know enough to maintain copies of important case files in unknown locations.

So I got the Gottlieb file and settled down to refresh myself, along with my scotch, of course. In the early interviews with Tiffany Market/Ann/Anne, when she described the murder scene on the bridge that snow-filled night, she'd said one of the men, a tallish figure, wore a dark old-fashioned fedora pulled well down on his head and a long dark overcoat.

Fine. It wasn't much to go on but when I saw that brief description and recalled the figure of a similarly dressed man in two recent locations, I began to get a prickle at the back of my head. Not hairs standing on end, exactly, just a niggle, a feeling. Was I being stalked by Manny Gottlieb's killer?

I set aside the file and went to the small bookcase. I was looking for my training manuals, the books by some of my favorite crime authors, Richard Prather and Wade Miller and Gil Brewer. Just then the doorbell chimed. I don't understand why we have one. The front doors to all the apartments have them, even though every visitor has to be welcomed by the security guard in the lobby. To be vetted the visitor gives a name and the name of the person visitor is visiting to the guard. He calls on the inside phone line and you agree to see whoever it is who's down there. There's also a private video channel so you can see, in black and white, who it is in the lobby. If the guard calls and there's no answer, the visitor doesn't get admitted. No going up in the elevator and ringing the doorbell to see if you can wake up somebody who might be dozing, or in the bathroom. If the guard doesn't get a response, the visitor can leave, or can wait a while and try again. Sometimes the guard would tell the visitor that the person wanted isn't in. The guards didn't always know that, unless the resident informed the guard or he saw the resident departing.

I knew all this because when I started seeing Catherine on a regular basis I wanted to know about security. It only took a few minutes to get to our apartment door from the lobby, even if the elevator wasn't right there, waiting. Which it always was.

So, nobody got to a residents front doors if they weren't home, or not answering, or someone whispered to the guard to send the visitor away with some other excuse. Nobody needed a doorbell. Sometimes Catherine hit it when she came home. Just to see if it still worked, I guess. She wouldn't tell me why she rang the doorbell when she came home from work. Maybe it was a warning so she wouldn't surprise me doing something naughty.

One day, she rang the bell because it turned out she'd forgotten her door key and I stripped off all my clothes and ran to the front door out of the bedroom to greet her, totally naked. She had a lawyer friend with her. My sudden appearance sans drapery evoked a momentary stunned look and then peals of laughter from both women. The entire evening was punctuated with semi-hysterical giggling and laughter. I'd look up and catch Joyce looking at me. She'd see me looking at her and suddenly giggle, which would set off Catherine. Frankly, I wasn't ever sure what the glances and giggles were all about and Catherine refused categorically to elucidate. I never did that again.

Anyway, the doorbell chimed and the door opened and my companion, Catherine Mckerney, sashayed in. After exchanging greetings, which involved a meeting of tongues, I said to Catherine I was going to the garage for a moment.

I left the apartment and traveled down to the basement garage with a brief stop at the security desk. In the cavernous dank place I did a discreet reconnoiter. The garage was secure, although not as tightly as the main entrance. There were a couple of cameras on electric-powered gimbals that scanned the space, but if you were sharp and spent a little time watching, you could find a way to get into the garage without being spotted. I had done it just to prove to myself it was possible. That little task had also satisfied me that my skills were still reasonably sharp.

Finding no causes for alarm, I rose again to our place, changed and went for a nice swim in the building's indoor pool. No one talked to me. Later, relaxing with a drink of fine single malt, I related the day's happenings to my apartment mate.

"Do you believe this man you've been noticing is really following you about the city?" Catherine queried.

"I don't know. You know I usually get a feeling about such and in the past we've both had a sense somebody was taking too much interest in us. But not with this guy, except that one time at the library where I had a strong feeling of being observed, but I couldn't detect the observer."

"I'll be extra watchful until you solve this case," she said.

I nodded and drained my glass. "That would be wise." Rising from my chair, I wandered into the kitchen with our glasses and went then to the dining room window. We had a light on in the kitchen and in the living room, but the dining room was darker. When I stepped to the window I looked out toward a part of the Minneapolis's downtown concentration of office and apartment towers. Many lights of traffic, streetlights, windows, spilt beams into the snowy streets and when I looked down there was somebody standing across the street from our building. Now in February one rarely saw people standing idly on the streets. They were most often hunched against the cold and hurrying toward their destination. About the only exception was for people watching the Winter Carnival parades in Saint Paul.

The figure lit a cigarette, which was how I happened to notice him. No, he wasn't wearing a fedora or a long coat and he appeared to have a backpack slung over one shoulder. No warning vibes, just a view of some guy on the street, smoking a cigarette on a sub-zero February evening.

Chapter 32

If I was being stalked and targeted by people involved with the murder of Mr. Gottlieb, it stood to reason the people doing said stalking were somehow associated with the Murchison clan. The only other very remote possibility was a third party, someone out of my past bent on righting some perceived wrong.

That seemed unlikely so I lasered in on the Murchisons. My first choice was the old man, Al, who had started this whole thing by apparently "liberating" the painting in question while he was stationed in Poland. I already had a file on him and I spent a few days asking around discreetly while also keeping an eye on my back trail. I had started watching for the tall dude in the old fashioned fedora, but he didn't come back for an encore.

A lawyer I knew contacted me for a possible insurance fraud gig. Over lunch I found out he had some peripheral knowledge of the Murchison clan. Minneapolis wasn't that big a town so people generally knew or knew about a lot of other people, especially those in the same line of work.

"I think the old man is retiring from the business. Leastways that's what I hear. They have a place in Florida. On one of the keys, I guess." He drank from his stemmed glass of chardonnay. We were doing lunch in a real restaurant with table covers and napkins of white cloth.

"The story is he's not too fond of his son, Al. Thinks he hasn't the stones to take over the running of the plant."

"Why don't they kick him upstairs to higher management?" I drank from my own glass of wine. The lawyer had ordered for both of us. I don't usually drink chardonnay. It's too fruity. "I mean Al. The son."

"You got me."

I didn't have him and I was getting a little impatient. So I pressed the lawyer and we came to terms and I was getting ready up to leave when the guy said, "I guess you know about the scandal, right?"

Since this was news to me, I sat right down again and stared into the lawyer's face. His eyes narrowed under my look and I raised one of my eyebrows. I forget which one.

"No," I said. "Tell me."

"Nothing you can take to court, you understand, but the story is the kid, Clem, may not be young Al's true son."

"This is a big deal?" Did I care if the Murchison men and women had been screwing around sometime in the past? You bet I did. Or might. But I wasn't going to give this attorney-client a clue to my level of interest if I could help it. He had a loose lip and I knew my business would soon be in the ears of others. I'd already revealed more about me to him than I was comfortable with.

"Oh, probably not, but the story is that the old man found his daughter-in-law in *flagrante delicto* as they say. I heard they were doin' the nasty at the plant." The attorney smirked and blotted a little wine from his lips. I was beginning to wish we hadn't come to terms on the insurance gig.

"So the story is the old man cold cocked both of them, sent the guy to the emergency room and then paid him off to keep him quiet. Then, about nine months or so later, the wife in question was delivered of a bouncing baby boy they named Clem."

I raised both eyebrows. "No abortion? And why don't they do DNA to clear things permanently?"

The attorney shrugged. "Dunno, but I'm betting they prefer not to know in case the kid's father is not a Murchison."

I left to make some notes in private and to hope there would be no possible way I would use this information about the marital peccadilloes of anybody in that family. I had several other questions to follow up on regarding these new nuggets of information. But I wasn't about to question Lawyer Loose Lips any further, thereby revealing my level of interest in the clan Murchison. As it was, I expected he'd tell his office mates about our lunch date and however he assessed the value of my interest in what I was now coming to call the Murchison affair.

In my office, while the dimness of the day outside grew. My hands were busy at routine tasks while a part of my mind shuffled through the new information I'd collected about the Murchisons. Then I decided to label it gossip for the time being. I had a few tasks to pursue that involved keeping my business going, such as sending out a few bills and making some follow-up calls.

Eventually I cleaned up my agenda and decided to turn my jaundiced eye on a Murchison. For no particular reason, I chose Alvin the current president. A quick drive by the plant revealed that his parking slot was empty. I drove to their neighborhood in Minnetonka Mills and discovered nothing. A light snowfall that morning lay undisturbed late this day on the driveway that pierced a gap between tall Colorado blue spruce and went on long enough that I had no sight of human habitation. I drove on up the road until I came to a small commercial district and an honest-to-god restaurant that wasn't a chain. I had no particular reason to stop at this establishment except it was not far from Murchison's and I felt the need of a cup of coffee.

I suppose you'd call it a coffee shop. It was situated back from the road, the narrow end pointed at the street with the door on the long side, where the big parking area lay. I parked, went in and sat at the counter. A lot of investigators, I read, would sit in a booth and chat up the waitress as she came by. But I found over the years that waitresses were mostly on the move, whereas the person behind the counter, male or female, was often restricted in space, which made it easier to carry on a conversation and, in the process, learn a few things.

"Pretty quiet this afternoon."

"Pretty quiet most afternoons." The woman poured me a cup of coffee without asking and stood waiting for an order.

"What kind of pie do you have?" I asked.

"The usual. Apple, pecan, cherry and one piece of banana cream left."

"I guess I'll have that, banana—"

"—Cream," she finished. "I thought you looked like coffee and banana cream pie when you came in."

I nodded and pulled out my small notebook while Hilda went to dish up my pie. I knew her name was Hilda because she was wearing a name tag on her breast that said so. Somebody started moving pots around in the kitchen, behind the counter, but Hilda didn't react so I assumed she knew who it was. There were two old guys in a booth wearing heavy coats and old baseball-style caps. The one I could read said Cargill Feed on it. There were two ceramic cups of coffee on the table. Steam tendrils backlit by the light from the windows rose from the dark liquid.

Hilda slid a generous piece of pie in front of me and refilled my coffee. "You want whipped cream?" She was holding a pressurized can of stuff and I nodded. She squirted a thick white gob of real whipped cream on my pie and I nodded.

"So, what brings you out this way, stranger?" she asked over the sound of the whipped cream issuing from the nozzle of the can.

I glanced up and saw her lips curving into a small smile.

"Wal, muh horse needed a rest and some water," I drawled.

Her smile widened and she said, "Plenty of room at the hitchin' post out back."

"Zane Grey or Max Brand?" I indicated the edge of a dog-eared paperback on the shelf behind her.

She chuckled with obvious pleasure and said, "Son of a gun, a reader. Actually, neither. That's an OK Western Romance by some gal named Beth Williams. Not my usual, but it passes the time."

She went off to offer refills to the two men in the booth. I tore a page out of my notebook and printed the Murchison postal address on the sheet. When Hilda came back behind the counter I showed her the address. "That's the Murchison place just down the road here."

"I recognize it. You a cop?"

"Private," I said. "How come you know the address?"

She grinned fleetingly. "Back in the day, I had a small thing with Clem. We were young, barely out of high school. That's his address. Before he got married," she added.

I made a note and started to ask another question. That's when the big window facing the street blew apart and glass and buckshot flew all over the place.

Chapter 33

In the sudden hush following the double boom from the shotgun and the high crash of disintegrating plate glass, one of the men in the booth started cursing in a flat, rapid, shock-filled monotone. When I risked a glance in his direction, he was staring at his wrist, specked with glass and blood. I was splattered with glass and knew I'd been hit by some buckshot, but my winter coat had protected me from serious damage.

I crunched around and looked for Hilda. She was sprawled on the floor behind the counter, still clutching the handle of the now disintegrated glass coffee pot and staring at nothing. There was a lot of blood on her face and her uniform was spotted with glass and crockery that had been on the counter to my right, toward the window.

"Hilda," I yelled and jumped the counter. The contents of the coffee pot were splashed all over Hilda and the floor. She blinked. I pried the broken pot handle out of her fingers and looked up at a white, frightened-looking face that appeared from the back. "Call 911," I snapped. "Quick. Nine-one-one."

The kid disappeared and I could hear him screaming into the phone. I peered at Hilda's eyes. She was breathing rapidly and scrabbling her heels, trying to get up, I guess. Her shoes slipped in the liquid on the floor underfoot. I took her hand and said, "Hilda, talk. Say something. Where does it hurt? Are you shot?"

Hilda took a quick gulp of air and her fingers squeezed mine. Then she took a deeper breath and whispered, "My face. My face hurts."

I bent closer, ignoring the rising pandemonium in the café on the other side of the counter. Hilda had black and sparkly speckles all over her face from plate glass and the birdshot. Birdshot! Somewhere in my mind I registered that the guy with the shotgun had been firing birdshot. If it had been double-ought buckshot, we would all have been killed or seriously wounded. As it was, the place was a mess and several patrons and one waitress would probably carry bandages for a while and maybe some scars for a lot longer. I had birdshot in the back of one hand and a peppered overcoat. This was obviously an unplanned opportunistic effort. It gave me a noticeably higher level of anger at whoever was trying to take me out. That they were incompetent made no difference. Birdshot through a plate glass window. Nuts.

Police sirens came rapidly closer as I found a clean napkin and ran some warm water in a bowl. I carefully bathed most of the loose stuff off Hilda's face. Fortunately, only a few of the cuts would require medical attention, and that was at hand. Apparently a passing EMT truck realized they were needed and stopped to help. As the paramedic knelt beside me, Hilda whispered, "Tell Clem I'd like to beat his ass."

Another medical guy, who'd already taken care of the two men in the booth, pawed through my hair to be sure I wasn't carrying any glass or stray birdshot around. At the same time, a Hennepin County cop stationed himself in front of me and asked a blistering series of questions I couldn't answer. Twice I explained that I'd had my back turned when the blast came and I'd gone right away to help Hilda, rather than chasing the shooter.

Finally the cop slowed down and said, "So, I take it you didn't see who actually fired the shots and you can't identify the vehicle. Correct?"

"That's correct, officer."

"And what were you doing here this afternoon?"

I glanced toward Hilda, who was being helped onto a gurney. Apparently she was pretty shook up, understandable under the circumstances, and hadn't heard the last question from the cop. So I ducked it. I was almost certain the shooter had been trying for me, but I didn't want to complicate my life or that of any of the others here. I shrugged as if I had no clue, even though I was beginning to feel infected with a Jessica Fletcher virus. You know, she was the star of that TV series, a writer played by Angela Lansbury, who was always seeing people murdered around her so folks in real life got to saying if they saw Fletcher on the street, they'd cross a highway to avoid getting close to her.

Anyway, the cops let me go and I left. On the way to my place in Roseville, I twigged to what Hilda had whispered to me just as the medics and cops arrived. She'd given me a message for Clem Murchison. It wasn't a nice message and it seemed a little out of place, considering what she had just experienced.

Except.

Except that she had been talking directly to me and not to the other folks in the place. Not to the cops. She was the only one looking directly toward the window when the gunner had pulled the trigger. She must have seen and recognized the shooter. I thought that's what she was telling me, that it was Clem Murchison firing the shotgun at us. I figured I'd had enough of Clem's deadly games, and I decided I would deliver Hilda's message, personally.

So I went looking for Clem Murchison.

My first stop was back to the Murchison family palace, a couple of miles down the road from the diner. Much of the snow on the driveway had disappeared, but there was enough so I could see there were still no tracks. That was not unexpected. I knew he was married and had a home across town. I didn't actually stop, just rolled into the wide driveway, swung parallel to the street and paused long enough to be sure of what I was seeing.

I put my foot down and skidded off toward north Minneapolis and the Murchison manufacturing plant. I slewed into their parking lot and stopped with no regard for the white painted lines on the macadam. I did take my keys. There was a car in Clem's reserved slot, but I didn't recognize it. When I stormed into the lobby, the receptionist sort of shrank back from her desk as if she was about to bolt out of there.

"Clem Murchison's office, right?" I snarled.

She pointed toward the same office where I'd met him.

"He's not—"

I waved her off and stomped toward the closed door. It did occur to me he could be waiting in there at his desk with a more lethal weapon than the shotgun he'd employed a while ago at the diner. In stride, I hunched my shoulders and slammed into the door. It made a loud crack, which must have been the jamb splintering, and it swung wide open.

I lurched into an empty office. When I stooped and peered under the desk, he wasn't hiding there either. Since the door had slammed back against the wall, I deduced Clem Murchison was not present.

"Is he in the plant?"

The receptionist gaped at me, chin trembling, evidently trying to get her vocal cords working. Instead she rapidly shook her head, which dislodged a couple of bobby pins. They skittered onto the floor.

"I want his home address. Now!"

She started to object, but I cut off her protest by lunging toward her.

"Right now!"

The poor woman quailed under my bark and teetered back to her desk. She tapped a few keys and my target's address and phone number appeared on her computer screen. I borrowed one of her pens and a scrap of paper and scribbled down the information. I shouldn't have demanded it and she sure as hell shouldn't have given it to me, but there it was. Was I falling just a little bit out of control?

"Thanks," I said and ran out of the place.

Back in my car I buckled up while looking at the address and drove out of the parking lot. The address was in an upscale rural community just over the Ramsey line in Washington County. Not having invested in a GPS finder for my car, I mentally plotted a fast route north to the Interstate and then east to White Bear. After that, I'd check a map, because his location looked to be rural in nature. I swung onto the eastbound lanes of Interstate 694 and realized I was driving into a growing snowstorm, and the flurries had begun to turn the highway treacherous. Traffic was slowing down and by the time I got to the connection to Highway 61, traffic almost stalled in both lanes. I avoided a large orange DMV truck and swooned down the off ramp and started north on 61. I say started because clouds of snowflakes soon enveloped me and nearby cars. Since the temperatures were now hovering around twenty degrees, according to the radio announcer, ice was building up. Traffic slowed even more.

My adrenalin was pushing at my brain. My foot stuttered on the accelerator and I tailgated until the driver in front pulled to one side so I could squeeze by. It made no difference. Both lanes in both directions were clogged with vehicles as far as I could see. That wasn't very far. How much of a lead did that bastard Murchison have on me? Was he even headed home?

An hour later I had sweated through five slippery miles of sometimes blinding snow and uncertain adhesion to the pavement. The radio announced the temperature had fallen almost eleven more degrees and now hovered just above ten. My Taurus slithered onto the slightly inclined driveway of Clem Murchison's house. No plow had yet touched this pavement. I stopped two car lengths off the street, shut down the engine and stepped out. The house, dimly seen through the snow bursts, appeared to be well lit up inside. There were lights on both downstairs and in a couple of front rooms on the second floor.

No outside lights.

I closed the car door and started to trudge toward where the front door should be.

Chapter 34

A CRUST WAS FORMING ON the new snow but light as I was I still sank in far enough so the red tops of my tennis shoes were soon soaked. The snow clung to my socks where it promptly melted and ran down to my toes.

The driveway had been plowed days ago but not since today's snowfall. That was a clue I probably wouldn't find Murchison in residence. Nevertheless I persisted. After slogging almost a quarter mile by my calculation, I saw a shoveled path leading to my left and the front of the house. I brushed snow from my coat and slammed the doorknocker, shaped like a roaring tiger, against its metal plate. Twice.

There was no light over the front door so I was not prepared when the door was yanked open. Although I'd been recently shot at and run over, I didn't believe the violence aimed in my direction was waiting for me here. It wasn't.

The woman who opened the door with "What?" had tangled lank blond hair. She had a very generous bosom under a gray sweatshirt and darker athletic pants. There were dark sweat patches at her armpits and she had to tilt her chin up to stare me in the eyes. I was momentarily distracted, not being able to remember the last time I'd had a face-to-face talk with someone shorter than me.

"This is a helluvatime to come calling," she said. "Who are you?"

"Mrs. Murchison? I'm looking for your husband. Is he here?"

"Clem? Huh, you and a lot of others. Answer is the same as it's been all day. He ran out of here this morning about ten and I haven't seen or heard from him since."

"You've had other inquiries?"

She shrugged. "A few calls. The office. A contractor, somebody who didn't give a name." She took a breath and went on in a milder tone. "It's getting rotten out there. Whyn't you come in and I'll make some tea." She stepped back and beckoned me in. Then she stopped and said, "I suppose I ought to ask you your name."

"Sean Sean. I'm a private investigator."

"Ah, a private investigator. Of course."

"Yes, ma'am. It's urgent that I contact Mr. Murchison as soon as possible."

"You and the rest of the world. Today like other days recently. People calling to talk to Clem. Well, never mind the snow. C'mon with me. We'll go in the kitchen."

And so we did. Mrs. Murchison strode well ahead of me. The kitchen was larger than I expected. It looked like it had been enlarged and modernized with some serious stainless steel equipment, like a commercial range and a side-by-side refrigerator and freezer. The big hood over the range looked like it was capable of sucking all the air out of the kitchen. Maybe even a small child.

The woman was busy at the counter, and I could see a glass coffee-maker over her shoulder. Beside it was a teapot swaddled in a knit jacket. Steam swirled up from the spout. She poured two cups in generous mugs and turned around with one in her hand. In her other hand was a small black automatic hand gun. She eyed me steadily, not exactly pointing the thing at me, just in my direction. I figured by the casual way she was handling it, she was totally unfamiliar with such weapons, or the opposite. I hoped she knew how to handle it, it made her less dangerous.

"Now wait," I started and raised both hands, palms out.

"Persuade me why I shouldn't wing you and call the local cops."

"Let me show you my ID and that I'm unarmed."

She raised one eyebrow, a lot like I sometimes do, and waggled the gun. "Maybe you don't have a pistol but I wouldn't call you unarmed, exactly. All right, slowly get it out." She leaned forward and set the mug of tea on the island counter and slid to her left to keep the island between us.

I kept looking at her and ran my hand into the breast pocket of my coat and fingered out my ID wallet. I keep it in a separate folder from my regular wallet with my driver's license and my lone credit card. I leaned forward and set it beside the steaming cup of tea. I picked up the mug and stepped back a pace.

The woman pushed up to the counter and took the wallet. She stared at the ID and then picked through the pockets. Then she dropped it on the counter and turned around to the teapot. When she turned back, the pistol was out of sight and she held another cup and a slight smile.

"I guess you have to be legitimate. Who'd phony up a fake ID with a name like Sean Sean? Don't you have a middle name?"

"Sadly, not," I said. "Let me tell you why I came out here in this storm." I gestured at the stool to one side and she nodded, so I sat down. I rested both hands in plain sight cupped around my steaming mug. The heat felt good. "Your husband has some information about a certain painting. I need that information in order to complete a business transaction with an overseas buyer."

"It's that damn painting the old man gifted to MIA, isn't it?"

"Well, I can't say for sure we're referring to the same painting." I hesitated and took a sip of hot tea. I was winging it, making things up as I went along.

"I knew that painting was going to be trouble." She sort of went inside herself for a moment, then, "I don't know where he's got to." She stared at me balefully through the steam from her cup.

"When was the last time you saw him?"

She frowned minutely and said, "I already told you. This morning at breakfast. He said he'd be late and not to wait dinner. He said if he did get home before I laid supper, he'd be here, but not to count on him. He told me he was sorry but there was a lot of pressure at work."

She stopped and blinked once. Her voice had taken on the sing-song cadence of someone who had repeated those words many times and she probably no longer believed them.

"I'm sorry," I said softly. "You were having guests tonight?"

She nodded and swiped at her eyes with a tissue.

"All my information says he left the plant and was heading home about three."

"I was shopping between, oh, three-thirty and four. I suppose he could have come and gone during that time."

I was beginning to get the feeling we both knew that was exactly what had happened. "Why would he do that? Is he running from something?"

Mrs. Murchison raised her head from her tea cup and now her look had softened. Her tone softened as well. "Isn't he always? I suppose this time he's running from you." She blew out her breath. "Okay, I might as well say it. I'm pretty sure he did come home between three-thirty and four. After I put the groceries away I went to our bedroom to change." She waved toward the ceiling.

"It looked like a cyclone had hit it. There were clothes strewn everywhere and one of his suitcases is gone from the closet. The middle-sized one. So I figure either he's left me for good this time or he's on one of his business trips. You want some more tea?" Her voice had acquired a tremor. In spite of her hard-edged demeanor, it looked to me as if she was on the verge of dissolving after years of psychological abuse from her husband. I sensed that further questions would not help either of us.

"No, thank you." I stood. "I'm sorry to have bothered you this afternoon, but it is necessary that I locate your husband as soon as possible."

"He does that you know. Leaves home without warning. For some kind of business trip." She stopped and stared into her mug again. I knew there were no tea leaves to provide the answers she so obviously sought. "Well, try not to hurt him too bad when you find him." With that surprising statement, she rose, apparently intending to show me the door.

We walked back along the hall toward the front of the house. The door to what I guessed was an office or maybe a library stood open and the light was on. Naturally I slowed and glanced inside. On the desk was a small bound book about seven or eight by five inches. Like a small ledger. The cover appeared to be suede and there was a word on it I couldn't read. The lettering was yellow.

I started to ask about the book and then Mrs. Murchison saw me staring and stepped in front of me. She looked me in the eyes and gently closed the door. "I hope you find what you are looking for," she said. At the front door she shook my cold hand and ushered me out into into the winter night.

Chapter 35

Snow was still falling and blowing all around, sometimes so thick I could hardly see the highway. Other times the wind calmed and visibility was pretty good. Plows had been up and down the highway so the road was reasonably clear, if slick in spots. The temperature was falling which meant snow should cease pretty soon.

We were all moving, but not very fast. It took me more than an hour to get to my place in Roseville. The driveway was plowed shut but I bucked my ride through the ridge and made it into the garage. Along the way I realized I'd never gotten Mrs. Murchison's first name, although she'd responded to 'Mrs. Murchison,' readily enough. It seemed I was becoming paranoid about everybody's identification.

After a phone call to Catherine, I broiled a pork chop and threw together a salad out of some almost-over lettuce and raw veggies. I put my feet up, scratched a cat on the head and began to think about the Murchison's purloined painting and a murderer's location. The airport had closed to outgoing flights so he wasn't getting away from me that way, at least for a few hours. I didn't really think he'd book it out of town, unless he had some place specific to go. I had no concrete reason to believe that, except the old intuition. Of course, I had no real proof that Clem Murchison was a killer. I just knew it. In my gut.

It was after nine, but I picked up the telephone anyway. Mrs. Murchison answered on the third ring, so she hadn't been asleep. No surprise.

"It's Sean Sean, again," I said.

"Yes, Mr. Sean," she said. she sounded calmer, in charge of her emotions.

"Uh, I neglected to ask. Just for my records, you know. Will you tell me your first name, please?"

"No harm in that, I guess. My name is Frances, Fran, everybody calls me."

"Thank you. Does your family have a lake place? A cabin up north somewhere?" I said. Me and Parker.

"Yes we do. It's on Pelican Lake, not far outside of Brainerd."

"Near Breezy Point," I said.

"Across a small bay. We can look at their beach," she confirmed.

"Could he have gone there?"

"It's possible, the place is winterized, but why would he?"

I sighed into the phone. "I don't know, Mrs. Murchison, I'm just checking possibilities. One other thing. Do you speak or read a foreign language?"

Silence. Then, "What an odd question. I studied Spanish in high school but I've never used it so I guess the answer is no."

"I'm looking for a record book, you see. I think it's probably written in a foreign language. German, maybe. Like a small ledger." I stopped, having given her a wide opening.

After a pause she said, "I see."

We listened to each other breathing for a moment and the phone went dead.

* * * *

MORNING CAME LATE. The white sun shown through a high screen of clouds on a white city. The fresh snow lay thick on trees, wires, lawns and buildings. The muffled sounds of the city awakening included the heavy rumble of snow plows. After the plow opened my street, the kid up the block came and blew out my driveway. Radio news guys said that traffic was slow going around Minnesota but no roads were closed. I could go anywhere as long as I was patient. And careful. "Sean Sean is always careful," I muttered to myself.

I called Catherine to tell her I might have to be away for a few days. Then I packed a small bag.

I loaded the bag in the trunk along with a carryall with one shotgun, and a couple of large handguns. Ammunition for all three weapons went in also. I was loaded for bear.

By three that afternoon I had a headache from peering at endless vistas of flat, contrast-less snowscapes. Even with all the black-appearing pine trees which populate that part of Minnesota, the fresh snow and the sun made me squint all the time, dark glasses notwithstanding. The temperature had fallen to minus five degrees.

The parking lot at Breezy Point Convention Center was plowed out and almost empty. I parked and trudged east toward the lake shore. Based on what Mrs. Murchison had told me, and with the aid of some seriously high-powered binoculars, I was able to pick out two, possibly three large lodges on the eastern side of Pelican Lake that were candidates for the Murchison place. Sure, I had the exact address and my little GPS device had pin-pointed the location, but I wanted a look at the neighborhood before I made my sortie.

Wind from the lake was coming up and the day seemed to be getting shorter by the moment. If I didn't hurry I'd be skulking around unfamiliar terrain looking for a way into the Murchison lodge in the blackness of an overcast winter night. I picked up my binoculars and set out around the lake. An hour later I had determined exactly which lodge was the Murchison place. It wasn't all that difficult. A mailbox at the road edge, perched on a metal post, had the name neatly lettered on it. I also determined that the homes on either side were vacant, at least at the moment. I hoped to be in and out before the light went away all together.

There was enough snow on the ground that it was impossible for me to reconnoiter the place without leaving tracks, so I didn't worry about it. If the question ever came up I'd just do something weird, like tell the truth. The only tracks in the yard were wild ones, deer and something that might have been a fox or a dog or a coyote. A tracker, I'm not.

I peered through the tall glass doors at the rear, the ones that looked out over the private dock and the frozen lake. I could see pinpoints of lights from the lodge windows at Breezy Point. I was still of a mixed mind about doing a B&E. That is, I was until my eyes adjusted to the dark and I stared at the room behind the glass. It didn't look right. I couldn't put a finger on it, but the room looked messy, out of sorts. Not exactly ransacked, just, messy. My flashlight, never the best, had died from the cold and lack of replacement batteries. My breath bloomed on the glass and obscured the room even more. I moved on around the house. There was no question of trying to break through the glass doors. They were tall, heavy, well-secured and made of three-paned weather-resistant glass.

At the north side of the house, I found what I needed. The door appeared to open on a mud room. It was an ordinary door with a single thermal pane of glass. I peered at the latch and lock. Ordinarily I'd have whipped out my tool kit of picks and so forth, something every well-equipped P.I. carried, right? I had a set of lock picks, but they were in the car and it was too cold to wade back through knee-deep snow to get them. I reared up with my well-padded elbow and smote the window a mighty blow. The pane shattered and my questing fingers found the deadbolt. I pulled the door open and sidled inside.

I'd been right in my assumption. The door opened on a mud room. There were pegs holding all manner of slickers, there were towels piled on hampers, and there were rubber boots lined up against one wall. I wasted little time looking and went up a couple of steps into the kitchen. Unlike the mud room I'd just left, the kitchen was tidy and closed down. The refrigerator was dark and the big gas range was cold and black. The counters were bare. This was a kitchen closed up for the season.

My ears tuned for any odd sounds other than those of my own making, I went forward into the next room which was obviously the dining room. Now that there were more windows, the outside light, even though fast disappearing, gave me enough to see there was a thin film of dust on the bare wood table.

I skirted the table and stepped into the next room. This was the room I'd peered into from outside the tall French-style window/doors. My impression had been right. This room was disturbed. Pillows lay helter-skelter on the floor and there was a sleeping bag tossed on one of the three couches that formed a misshapen ring around the fireplace. I bent down over the mound of ashes in the fireplace. They smelled like you'd expect. Wood ashes. Cold, ordinary. This fire had been out for several hours if not days.

At that moment I heard a faint click and the atmosphere of the room changed. I started to crouch down to the floor when I realized what had just happened. Listening harder, I heard the faint sound of a well-muffled fan. Somewhere in the place a furnace had just kicked on and the hot-air fan had started. It confirmed what I had suspected. When the Murchisons closed up the place, they left the furnace set to a temperature that kept the pipes from freezing. But when somebody came in, say an interloper, he might not want to heat the whole place, so he had a fire in the fireplace, and snuggled down in a sleeping bag. So where was my mysterious interloper and who was he?

I moved on to a door in the wall beside the fireplace. It led to a hall. I knew that because the door was partly open and I could see along the hall to the opposite side of the house. There was also a closed door in that same wall which I assumed would reveal an office or some other kind of room. A library, perhaps. I opened the door to discover my assumption was correct. It was obviously an office. There was also a body on the floor.

Chapter 36

There was no question in my mind the guy was dead. But just to be sure I leaned over and pressed my fingers against the carotid artery in his neck. His skin was cold to the touch and he had no pulse. Ergo . . .

I didn't recognize the guy. Peering at the body through the gloom I realized I had a new dilemma, a dilemma and more questions. The DB wasn't Clem Murchison. His blocky shape, even allowing for a winter coat was wrong. Who the hell was this? Sprawled out on his face, I had to lean over to get a good look at him. I peered at his chin, it was clear he hadn't shaved in a few days. He was cold to the touch and didn't smell so he hadn't been dead too long.

What I should do was trudge out to the car, find a phone and call the local cops. If I did that and waited around, I'd have some explaining to do and I'd spend a lot of time doing it, always assuming I could persuade some deputy or the sheriff himself, that I was an innocent bystander, guilty of nothing more than innocent breaking and entering.

I stared at the scene for a few moments more to sort of fix things in my head, in case questions came up. My digital SLR always seems to be somewhere else. The dead guy was sprawled on his face beside the desk on which I observed nothing, except a few smudges in the dust. It looked like my dead body when alive, or someone else, had been interrupted in a search. None of the drawers of the desk, which were locked, appeared to have been jimmied. I scanned the room. Nothing appeared out of place. There were drag marks in the dust on the floor that sort of pointed to the side where my DB lay. I figured the marks occurred when this guy fell over. I examined his outer clothes.

He was dressed in a heavy dark overcoat. It felt like wool that had seen better days. I rolled him over. He'd missed a hole when he buttoned up. The legs of the deceased below the hem of the coat were encased in what looked like dark heavy denim and he wore low boots with thick soles. Workingman's boots. On the floor beside his head was a black billed cap. Not like our baseball caps. This was the kind of billed cap you sometimes see on farmers working in the fields of Europe. This DB might be the third man, the one who actually threw Mr. Gottlieb off the stone arch bridge in Minneapolis, as described to me by that woman, Ann/Anne. I decided I needed to look at him more closely.

I sidled back into the living room. On a small shelf beside the fireplace I found a box of old fashioned kitchen matches. A hum came to my ears and a ghostly light flickered over the hearth. I looked toward the front of the property to see the blurry glow of headlights going down the road. If that was a concerned citizen, I might not have more than a few minutes before a nosy deputy showed up asking impertinent questions.

I needed a light of some kind. I grabbed the matches and a section of newspaper and scuttled back to the DB. It hadn't moved. With the aid of a match or two and a torch fashioned of tightly twisted newsprint, I determined that the dust on the floor had been seriously tracked and disturbed, probably in a scuffle, so my presence might be overlooked. I slid my fingers into the DB's pockets, looking for anything that might tell me who he was. Nothing, zip. I pulled off one shoe. He had a hundred dollar bill folded under the sole of his left foot. His other shoe, except for sock and foot, was empty. I replaced the hundred.

I decided it was time to skedaddle. I would have liked very much to search the house, but I had to hope that the citizen who'd just driven past my car on the road hadn't noted my license plate. I took my burnt matches and scraped up the ashes from the section of newspaper and crammed the mess into my side pocket. Then I beat it out of there. I took the time to wedge the mud-room door shut and retraced my footprints in the snow back to the road. As I fired up my Taurus, I looked both ways along the dark empty road and at the somber colorless forest. Then I drove slowly south.

In Little Falls, I stopped and found a pay phone. I called the Crow Wing County Sheriff to report suspicious goings on near the lodges along the lake across from the Breezy Point Resort. When the person at the sheriff's office became insistent and started asking pointed questions I wasn't prepared to answer, I gently hung up. By midnight, I was wearily unloading my arsenal through the garage and contemplating a good slug of scotch and a warm bed.

* * * *

DAWN CAME FAR TOO SOON after a restless night. Damn it! What exactly had I learned? Or accomplished? In hindsight I thought now I could have just stayed on and searched the whole place for whatever I might find, hoping for something that would lead me to Murchison. Instead, now I had to deal at long range with finding that body. The more I thought about it the more convinced I was that the DB was one of the men on the bridge Ann/Anne had described to me.

The snow had stopped overnight but the gray clouds seemed lower and denser. I made it to my office without incident. I contemplated calling Mrs. Murchison to tell her I hadn't located her husband. But what if she asked me whether I went up north to their lake place? She had no reason to, except I'd asked her earlier if they had a lake cabin and she might remember. I could lie, of course, stock in trade for the nimble P.I. My decision was to avoid her for the time being. The overcast day was getting to me again. Or still. Time for a careful review.

Seeking answers to the circumstances surrounding the murder of Aaron Gottlieb's great uncle, Manfred, I had encountered a woman who said she witnessed the murder. Her name, she told me was Anne or Ann. Because she didn't spell it, I wasn't sure. Truth to tell, I was no longer sure if that was her real name at all. When I had earlier pressed her on her involvement, I learned she had been on the bridge and had seen Manny Gottlieb killed. She, I subsequently learned, had picked up a small package, a bound ledger-like book written in German script, which turned out to be a list of valuables, jewelry, art, like that.

At one point, a man who said his name was Robert Gehrz showed up. A very slick dude. He was paying me to find a woman whom he called Tiffany Market. He gave me a little song and dance about the woman he was dating. Tiffany Market. She had disappeared, he told me, hadn't shown up for a date after their relationship had become well-established, according to Gehrz. It hadn't taken me very long to decide that the woman in white, Ann/Anne and Ms. Market were the same person. But why the different names? I didn't like it when people ran games on me, or tried to. That was my gig.

Then it occurred to me this whole ploy could be a game Gehrz was running. Maybe he was trying to determine how effectively the woman had stayed out of sight and off the usual radar screens. But why? How bizarre was that? Unless he and she were seriously worried about her safety. Sort of a small witness protection scheme. In the midst of my ruminations, I called the contact number I had for Gehrz. Naturally no one answered, but a hollow-sounding voice announced I could leave a message so I did.

All right. The timing for all this was coincidental, or, looked at from a different perspective, precisely on the mark. The little twist in the Gehrz-Market-Ann/Anne triangle is that I knew now that the females were one and the same and it appeared Gehrz was backstopping the woman. My gut told me I was on the right track. What my gut didn't tell me was why this was happening. Was it only because she witnessed a murder and wouldn't come forth, even though she was clearly anxious to have the murderers caught? But she wouldn't come forward. Why not? The only reason I could think that makes sense was that she was following one of the people on the bridge. Either she was shadowing Manny, or the two murderers. This was all based on my gut feeling that Ann/Anne, otherwise known as Tiffany Market, was the very same individual. Ah, now we come to something quite interesting and for me, unsettling.

Just suppose, I considered, this woman in white was there on the bridge, following the two thugs she claimed murdered Gottlieb because they were all somehow involved in a wider conspiracy. Perhaps she was connected in some way with an international agency. Oh, crap. I did not want to be involved in any way with this kind of situation. I put international crime right up there with the mob, the Mafia, organized crime. The kind of stuff that could get you too easily snuffed for no rational reason. In spite of my attitude, it appeared I was trapped.

This raised the question of why and how my home-town miscreants, the Murchison gang, was involved. There was only one possibility I could see. The damn Neumann painting now hanging at the MIA must be the connection. I was betting that somewhere in the pages of that little brown ledger was a reference to that painting and, therefore, who owned it, who confiscated it and who was, therefore, implicated in thievery and murder.

How implicated, I asked myself?

My assumptions suggested that Old Man Murchison stole the painting, that is to say, in the parlance of the times, he liberated the painting from a stash probably collected originally by the SS. He rolled it up and brought it home where he used it as collateral for a loan to buy into a machine shop on the north side of Minneapolis. That which now goes by the name of Murchison Machinery.

Lately, there had been some publicity about valuable paintings and other artwork being in the possession of institutions and private individuals but without adequate provenance. Like bills of sale. Or wills, or letters of transfer. Now, in the old days, during the time of empire building, certain powerful companies and individuals went marauding through foreign countrysides and when they unearthed art works of interest, carted them home to help enlarge national museums of one sort or other. Some, like the sphinx, were too large to transport, but the carting off of subjugated nation's heritage was sort of normal, at least to the victors. Today we tended to think of that as plain old robbery.

In a few recent cases museums have graciously returned to heirs objects found to have been stolen. Such, I suspected, was the circumstance surrounding the Neumann painting. Once the piece was donated to MIA without adequate provenance, MIA officials began a process to find the true owner. Somehow, that triggered the tragic murder of Manfred Gottlieb. Wait a minute. Maybe the painting was only a part of this picture. Could I have been going at this the wrong way? What if Murchison was a player but not the prime mover? Suppose it's not the painting but the missing ledger that was the real focus and the motive for the murder of Manny Gottleib?

Was I back to square one? The door opened and in sashayed Belinda Revulon from down the hall. She carried a thick brown envelope of the document size.

"Hey, Sean. This got mis-delivered."

She handed me the envelope and sashayed back out the door with a little hip bump and finger wiggle.

The package was from Aaron Gottlieb in Chicago. Inside were fresh photocopies of sheets of a diary in Polish and English. The note from Aaron confirmed they were parts of Manny's diary, along with a translation. It was that little brown ledger. What I learned was that Manfred Gottlieb returned to his home along the Bug River and found a lot of rubble and a book in a slipcase. A ledger.

Now I could develop a logical scenario. The gift of the painting to MIA, which triggered a search for provenance, in turn created a ripple or two inside Derrol Madison's organization, Atria. Somehow, those ripples revealed that Manny Gottlieb had in his possession a ledger that contained information about the SS theft of art works in far off Poland during the early part of World War Two. If the ledger turned up and was authenticated, a lot of prominent people elsewhere in the world might see their lives and reputations trashed. The solution was to locate and destroy the ledger, or use it as primary evidence to seek out and arrest the perpetrators of the thefts to which the ledger would testify. Even the copies of a few pages that I had, were of little use without the original. It looked to me like my mysterious woman in white, Ann/Anne had the ledger, was sending me copies of pages to keep me interested in catching Manny's killers, all while using me to preserve her wall of secrecy. Gehrz was in the picture to backstop the bogus Tiffany Market.

By now I was grinding my teeth, but my way was clearer. Find Ann/Anne and lay hands on the ledger. I grabbed the phone and called the Murchison home.

"Fran Murchison," she answered.

"Mrs. Murchison. Good morning. It's Sean Sean. I have an impertinent question."

"Okay."

"When I was at your home, I noticed a small gray or brown book on the desk. It appeared to have gold or yellow lettering on the cover. Am I correct?"

"Yes. So?"

"What is it?

"It's actually a ledger. You can buy them in bookstores. Some of them come in a slipcase. D'you know what that is?

"Yes, ma'am."

"I keep my household financial records in it. Why?"

"It reminded me of something I can't quite put my finger on, that's all." I wasn't about to tell her it looked a lot like it belonged to the slipcase I'd found at the Gottlieb house. "I don't suppose you've heard from your husband since last we talked?"

"Right. I haven't." She sighed and abruptly hung up.

I called Darrol Madison.

"I'm updating you. As you know, German agents kept meticulous records of the goods they appropriated from people they conquered."

"That's correct."

"It looks like some of those records, in the form of a ledger have shown up here in Minneapolis."

I knew I wasn't telling the lawyer anything he didn't already know or suspect. I was mainly interested in his reaction to my knowing. He didn't say anything for a moment.

"Mr. Madison?"

"Do I understand you to mean you've seen or got your hands on such a ledger?"

"Not exactly."

"Perhaps you should explain."

"I'm pretty sure the woman I told you about, Ann/Anne with no last name, has possession of one such ledger."

"I see. You know this how?"

"She's been supplying me with copies of pages."

Madison's voice took on a sharper tone. "What's on the pages?"

"The translation I have so far mentions furniture and household utensils. Why would they confiscate furniture?"

"We aren't sure. Some of it may have been valuable but we think some of it may just be a result of over-zealousness on the part of nervous lower ranks. Is there any chance you can get your hands on the original pages?"

"I don't know. I'm working on it. Have you any rumblings of representatives from outside law enforcement taking an interest?"

"Not locally. It does happen. Once in a while one of our inquiries provokes the CIA or the FBI. I'm not aware of anything local at the moment."

I paused and made a decision. "Look. I've been on the wrong track I think. It isn't the painting at all. The one at MIA that Murchison donated. I think the old man, Gottlieb, came home from Poland after the war with a written record of German thefts stashed in his belongings. It was a small handwritten ledger in a slipcase. Brown with gold embossed lettering. Somehow, somebody got wind of it and came looking because somebody else is worried about what may be in the ledger. I think that when Manny Gottlieb wouldn't turn it over to a pair of thugs, he was killed."

"But why? Those ledgers exist. You can even see pictures of them on the Internet. They certainly aren't worth killing for."

"Are you sure about that, Mr. Madison? I think the gift of the painting to the MIA and the gallery's subsequent decision to repatriate it, set off an alarm somewhere. I believe there are people out there who are afraid of what's in the ledger and want it destroyed. If Anne's statement to me is accurate, two men accosted Gottleib on the bridge and threw him into the river. She picked up the ledger and is keeping it safe somewhere. Now I also think that slick operator, Gehrz, showed up to see that her cover wasn't penetrated by somebody. By anybody. I'll be surprised if we don't discover that both Anne and Gehrz are foreign agents of some kind.

"I'm willing to bet the two guys who killed Gottleib are foreign operators as well. I'm also pretty sure one of them is dead."

"What?"

"That's right. Never mind how I know or the circumstances. I'm telling you this so you can decide how you want to proceed."

"Dammit," he said softly in my ear. "All right, I appreciate the heads up. What's your next move?"

"I haven't figured that out yet." I hung up the receiver. I'd be damned if I'd give him any clue. He might be on the side of the angels, but I didn't know who he talked to. I knew exactly what I had to do next, apart from avoiding getting arrested or killed.

Chapter 37

I went downstairs and got a paper cup of bad coffee from the kiosk in the corner of the lobby. The guy who ran the place had been there when I moved in ten years earlier and people who'd been in the building a lot longer said he probably came with the place when it was first built. But that was in the late thirties of a previous century, so I kind of doubted that. He did look old enough to have been there since the end of the Korean War. He moved slow and his coffee wasn't very good, but it was hot and fresh any time he was open so that was something.

Back in my office I called my good buddy Sergeant Ricardo Simon. For a change, he was at his desk. "How's your day?" I asked.

"'Bout the same as yesterday."

"I'm calling to find out what you've learned about that stash of papers we picked up in the basement the other night." I was sure there was no need to remind Ricardo to which basement I was referring.

"Interesting you should ask, just now. What do you know about a dead body found late last night up on Pelican Lake?"

"Almost nothing. Why would I?"

"I don't know, but we've had an inquiry from the county sheriff."

Rats. Somebody talked out of turn or my car was traced. "I have nothing to say to that."

We enjoyed a moment of mutual silence and then Ricardo went on. "Ah. Well, I have been formally advised, although not in writing, to forget about that envelope of papers."

"Really?"

"Really. I haven't even been asked for the source of my advice, so you won't get a formal cease and desist order. I sort of scanned through them and sent the package to forensics. Then I got the message to lay off. I guess somebody in the lab saw something that triggered a call. You take my meaning? Between me and them, I suspect the well-manicured fingers of people far above me in pay grade, even people who live in other states, are now involved."

"You're starting to talk funny. I was hoping for a quid pro quo here, but I guess that's not in the cards, either, yes?"

"Sean, we, or rather you, seem to have stepped in something. And I get the feeling we do not want any of it sticking to our shoes."

"Yeah," I said. "It's probably international in scope. I bet the body in Crow Wing County turns out not to be a citizen. I also bet he had something to do with Manny Gottlieb."

"Shit. I thought you just denied all knowledge of that body."

"Not all, my friend. Plus, there are a lot of things I'd like to know about him. Like for example, who were his associates and where are they?"

Ricardo didn't say anything for a minute then, "You got any rational basis for suggesting a dead guy in Crow Wing County is somehow linked to Manny Gottlieb's murder here in Hennepin County?"

"I expect the location of the dead guy turns out to be a place belonging to Murchison Manufacturing."

"Almost right," said Ricardo.

I shifted the phone to my other ear. "Almost right?"

"Murchison Engineering is the property owner of record."

"Oh, well, I guess that makes all the difference in the world, yes?"

Simon chuckled. "It may. Gotta go. Try to stay out of trouble."

"Keep in touch," I responded, hanging up.

There was a rap on the doorjamb of my office. The door swung slowly open and I looked up to see a face I'd hoped I'd never see again. Robert Gehrz lounged there, his coat open, his hat pushed back on his head. For the buttoned-up dude I'd encountered in earlier days, this man looked almost disheveled, relaxed, even. His suit coat was unfastened and his tie was slightly askew. Ever since Gehrz had entered my life I'd had a crawly feeling he linked me to some criminal stuff way above my competence level.

"Mr. Gehrz. I didn't expect to see you again, ever," I said. I pulled my chair closer to the desk, dropping one hand into my lap, fingers closer to the pistol in the holster strapped to the wall of the kneehole in my desk. I hadn't had to use the quick release lever on the holster for months. I hoped the lever still worked as smoothly as when I installed it.

"Sorry, I didn't call first to make an appointment, but I'm a little short of time here. I just came to settle our account. I believe I owe you a final payment for locating my friend."

"Since I didn't actually put you two together, physically, I can't claim success. But you do owe me for some additional expenses. Say five hundred? You could have just mailed me a check if being here is inconvenient."

That remark passed without a response. Gehrz stepped into my office and came to the desk. "Five hundred will be quite satisfactory." He fished out an envelope that looked exactly like the one he'd displayed on two previous occasions. From the envelope, he produced five one-hundred dollar bills. They looked exactly like those he had handed over at our most recent meeting. Holding them gingerly by the very edges, he laid them on my desk in front of me. Gehrz showed a tiny smile that lifted one corner of his mouth a millimeter or two. It was as if he was demonstrating a technique. Maybe something he learned in spy school.

"Thank you," I said. "Do you want a receipt?"

No response. Gehrz merely raised one eyebrow. I wasn't in the habit of giving out receipts, but it seemed appropriate to ask. Apparently not so.

"I expect we won't be seeing each other again," he said then, "but should that happen, I hope I can count on your discretion."

"Of course. Goodbye." We didn't offer to shake hands. Gehrz turned and left my office without closing the door. I could hear his measured steps down the empty hall. I heard the elevator door open and close. Robert Gehrz was out of my life forever. I hoped.

* * * *

MY PHONE RANG THIRTY MINUTES later, just as I was packing up to go home. I'd cleaned out my office files of everything relating to the Gottlieb-Gehrz-Market-Murchison business. Two thick envelopes, sealed and addressed to my occasionally used rented post office box were on my desk. I intended to deposit them with the Revulon sisters down the hall for their mail pickup later in the day. I would enjoy a late afternoon and an evening with my lady. No worries. The phone call was a wrong number.

Chapter 38

Arriving at my office around eleven the following morning, I discovered there had been no break-in, no one had left a message on my answering machine, and the mail contained no mystifying letters or packages. Things were entirely too calm.

My ruminations had pretty well tied up the case except for a couple of vital areas. There was still the question of who was responsible for the multiple attempts on my life, by truck and by birdshot, although Clem Murchison was becoming a serious person of interest in that regard. I did wonder what had happened to change Mr. Gehrz so significantly. Every time I'd seen him until yesterday, he'd been one buttoned-up dude, at least sartorially. Maybe it became just another question in this case. This case. I was beginning to believe I wasn't ever going to answer my questions with any satisfaction. Not entirely unknown. More than one of my cases ended with some questions unanswered. Many times the lack of information went to motive. But here, I was almost overwhelmed with questions that lacked answers. It irked me.

My telephone alerted me to an incoming call. It turned out to be somebody from the Minneapolis Fire Department's arson investigator.

"Mr. Sean. I'm following up with some information for you regarding the fire at that address on Forty-sixth. The former Gottlieb residence."

"Yes. And thank you for the call. What have you learned?"

"We're quite sure it's a case of arson. Investigators found traces of an accelerant in the attic. But it has the appearance of a half-hearted effort, if I may use that expression."

"I'm not sure what you mean."

"If I had to guess, and this is certainly not for public consumption, I'd suggest whoever set this fire, wasn't especially interested in destroying the house, just the attic. Because of circumstances, we got the call early and responded quickly, so damage was limited even more."

"Who called it in?" I wanted to know.

"According to my information, an unnamed civic-minded passerby."

"Really."

I could almost see the smile on the investigator's face. "Yep. An anonymous male reported smoke in the attic as seen from the street. He didn't give a name or where he was when he called it in. He said he saw clouds of smoke through the attic window."

"I believe there are windows on two sides," I said.

"Correct. When the truck arrived a battalion chief reported they were delayed a few moments because none of the crew could see smoke from the street and the address numbers had been removed from the front of the house at some time in the past."

"I get it. You are perhaps assuming the caller didn't actually see smoke, but knew it was there because . . ." I let my voice trail off.

"That is consistent with my thinking."

"Interesting. Anything else you'd care to tell me?"

"Not at this time, Mr. Sean. But should you develop any new information, we'd appreciate it if you'd get in touch with the arson investigation office."

"Count on it," I said and put the hand piece in the cradle. Unable to lay hands on the ledger, the thieves or thief had tried to insure the ledger would be destroyed. Perhaps because they were not experienced in arson, they misjudged the thing and the prompt arrival of the fire department prevented the house from burning to the ground. I was willing to bet, though not a large sum, that it wasn't the arsonist, but somebody who was shadowing the arsonist, who called the fire department. That suggested one Robert Gehrz. But it could easily have been someone else, perhaps the someone else who killed the Crow Wing guy. No matter how I twisted the known facts, I couldn't paint Gehrz with that killing. It just wasn't his style.

It was beginning to look very much as if the people who murdered Gottlieb were leading a parade of foreign agents around my city. If I could nail the killers, maybe the rest of those people would disappear. Meanwhile, where was Clem Murchison?

The phone rang. It was Mrs. Clem Murchison. "I just heard from my husband," she said with no preamble.

"Did he tell you where he is?"

"He's in the basement."

"Excuse me?

She laughed but there was no mirth in the sound. "News to me too. I answered the phone a minute ago and it was him. He said he'd been up at the lake and encountered a spot of trouble. His words."

The image of the dead guy in their cabin rose in my mind.

"When I asked him when he'd be home, he said he was in the apartment in the basement. Our basement here. He warned me not to come down. I don't know why."

"How'd he sound?"

"Desperate, I guess I'd say. Despondent maybe?"

"All right. Stay put and I'll be there as quick as I can."

"Shouldn't I call the police?"

"Up to you, of course, but I'd really like to talk to him first."

Mrs. Murchison sighed in my ear and broke the connection. I dropped the instrument and grabbed my coat. Outside the back door I was met with a blast of snow and a snarling wind in my face. The trip to White Bear was going to be slow and fraught, I figured.

My prediction was right. The going was tediously slow. Once again the Murchison driveway was snow-filled with only faint indentations from car tracks. They were rapidly filling. I looked, but I couldn't discern how many vehicles had recently preceded me. In the parking area next to the front of the house a single black Mercedes with an inch of snow on the roof and hood sat as a lonely sentinel. I stomped up the front steps and hammered on the big door. Snow swirled around me and some of it melted into icy rivulets and ran down the back of my neck.

I never heard approaching footsteps so I was startled when the door was yanked open by the senior Murchison. CEO of Murchison Engineering. "What?" He snarled. "We don't need you here right now."

"Is that Mr. Sean?" The voice came from somewhere toward the back of the house. I recognized it as that of Mrs. Murchison. Clem's wife. "I called him. I want to talk to him."

Murchison senior growled something I didn't catch and turned away. He stalked rapidly back toward the source of the voice, leaving me to deal with the door and my outer wraps. My warning radar sent me siren signals. I dropped my wet coat and hat on the chair by the door and trotted toward the hall to the kitchen. There I found Fran Murchison looking somewhat distraught. She had a glass of what looked like gin or vodka on the kitchen counter, along with a cell phone. A second glass was empty. I assumed it belonged to Murchison.

"Do you want a drink?" Her voice was clear. She didn't slur, but the tension was thick and I smelled booze.

"No thanks. What's the situation?" I slid onto a stool.

Before she could answer, Murchison, senior, reappeared from a room off to the side. He looked and acted agitated. "The door's locked," he said.

"Door to the basement apartment," Fran Murchison supplied.

The old man sighed gustily and stared at me from under thick bushy white eyebrows. "If you hadn't started poking around, none of this would have happened."

"None of what?"

"I've always known my boy was a little high strung. He just went out of control here."

"Uh huh."

"Look, I'm trying to return the painting. Eventually it'll get back to the people it belongs to. Isn't that enough? God damn it!" Murchison slammed his hand onto the counter making a sharp loud crack. I flinched.

I stared at him. "Do you know who killed Mr. Gottlieb? And who's trying to take me out? It's your son, isn't it? We better call the cops."

"Hell you say! I'm going around the back to the outside door," said Murchison. "I'll get him out of there if I have to drag him." He barely glanced at me as he went by, hurrying through the house toward the front door.

"His relationship with Clem was always mixed. Sometimes he was protective, others he seemed to want to disown him," Fran muttered. "Now he's afraid what may have happened, of what Clem may have done."

"Have you talked with your husband since you called me?"

She shook her head and swallowed a healthy portion of whatever she had in the glass.

"It was Clem who shot at me in the diner, wasn't it."

She shrugged. "Call the police if you think that." It wasn't an admission but I could see the truth of it in her face. Fran took another drink and looked me in the eyes. "Wait, please. Let Clem's father try to talk to him."

"You said he has a phone?" Getting through to her was becoming more and more difficult.

"Want some coffee?" Her words were becoming a little sloppy.

"I want to call your husband."

She reached behind her and brought out a small bright red cell phone, tapped in a number and handed it to me. "Just press send," she muttered. I did that.

The phone rang twice in my ear and then connected.

"What?"

"Mr. Murchison. It's the detective, Sean Sean. I'm here at the house. Upstairs. Don't you think it's time we talked?" In the background I heard a faint banging. The old man must be hammering on the outside door.

Murchison didn't say anything, but he didn't hang up either.

"Mr. Murchison? Clem? Why don't you come up and unlock the door? We really should talk. Things have a way of working out, don't you agree?" I wasn't sure what I was saying, or what things were going to work out, but I knew if Clem Murchison would talk to me, we might resolve the situation.

In the background there was the sound of glass breaking, a sharp rise in the volume of shouting. What I heard was No. No. and then the sounds of gunfire from two different weapons slammed through the phone and from the basement. I dropped the instrument, ran to the door off the kitchen and slammed my foot against the panel beside the knob. The door flew open and I pushed in, almost falling down the stairs to the basement. I went down two steps at a time, the acrid smell of burned gunpowder filling my nose. There was another shot.

I dropped to my knees. The stairs went straight down to a cement block wall so I had to make a right turn to see the whole basement. When I turned, I crouched lower, then dropped flat to the cold floor and rolled into the basement. Looking up past a counter, I saw old man Murchison slumped against the outside door frame. He was holding a snub-nosed revolver and there were two large spots of bright spreading blood on his white-shirted chest.

My inclination was to jump to his aid but where was his son? A harsh coughing-gurgle reached my ears from close above my head. Then there was a scraping sound and a shiny double-barreled shotgun slid off the counter overhead and fell to the floor. I stood up. Directly in front of me, half sitting on a stool and bent over was Clem Murchison. The shotgun had obviously fallen from his hands. I reached to his carotid artery. He had no pulse.

"Mrs. Murchison," I hollered up the stairs. "Call 911 right now." There was no response. I stepped around the son and went to the old man. Again the carotid artery and again, no pulse. The holes torn by the shotgun slugs had stopped oozing blood. Two Murchisons, father and son, both dead. Right then, I felt responsible.

I stared at the scene until I had the details burned into my brain. Murder suicide? I'd narrate a set of notes when I got back to the office sometime.

Then I went upstairs to a nearly drunk widow. "I'm sorry," I said to her. "Your husband and father-in-law are both dead down there. It looks like they shot each other." I left her there at the kitchen counter, clutching a glass now mostly empty of the clear liquid she'd been drinking. Through the muffling snowfall outside I could hear approaching sirens. Mrs. Murchison had apparently had the wit to call for help. I glanced into her office as I went toward the front door. On her desk among files and scattered papers, directly under the light from a banker's green-shaded lamp, was a small frayed book. It lay face-down and appeared to have had some hard handling. I took out a pen and flipped the book over. Embossed on the cover was the word "Beschlaghmen." It was identical to the word on the empty slipcase Aaron and I had found in his granduncle's attic. I slipped the book under my belt at my back and shrugged into my coat. Then I went to the door and opened it to the first responders.

Chapter 39

It was early February and colder than the proverbial. I was standing with my friend in a secure location at the Minneapolis/Saint Paul airport. From floor to ceiling in front of us were rows of high definition television screens. They were fed by cameras located throughout the building. This room was not part of the public terminal.

We watched as passengers and workers flowed back and forth from inside the secured section of the terminal.

"There," said my friend who'd pulled a number of strings to get me clearance to this room. He pointed at one screen high up near the ceiling. A tall slender man walking deliberately appeared from the direction of the terminal security wall operated by TSA. He headed down the concourse toward the International Terminal where passengers destined for overseas locations would gather to be screened again by Immigration authorities. He carried a top coat and a small travel case slung over one shoulder. Just before he left the camera view, Robert Gehrz turned and stared upward, as if he'd become aware of our scrutiny. When he stopped, a woman walking behind him seemed to stumble against him. Gehrz put out a hand and took her elbow. She turned her head and said something. So, Robert Gehrz had finally found the woman he'd told me he'd lost for a time, Ann/Anne/Tiffany Market.

I watched and wondered which of them had been responsible for the death of the Nazi criminals who murdered Manfred Gottlieb. Mr. Gottlieb had endured the loss of his home, his family, and incarceration in a prison camp, only to come to America and find death on a cold wintry night on a frozen river in Minnesota.

Days later, I would apologize to Aaron Gottlieb that I was unable to identify and bring to justice the murderers of his great uncle but that I was sure they had been appropriately dealt with. When I placed in his hands the ledger that Manfred had brought to Minnesota, the ledger that documented the theft of the Neumann painting and so much more thievery, and had led to the deaths of five people, he seemed mildly nonplussed. He thanked me for my services and went out of my office to go back to his family and his safe life in Chicago.

I put on my coat, shut off the lights and went home through snowy streets to my love.